READ THE BOOK, THEN CONTINUE
THE ADVENTURE ONLINE!

The Death Walkers are rising and bringing plagues
of evil to the world. It's up to YOU to stop them!

1. Go to scholastic.com/tombquest
2. Log in to create your character and enter the tombs
3. Have your book ready and enter the code below to play:

RDWWPW2GU2

MICHAEL NORTHROP

TOMBQUEST

THE STONE WARRIORS

SCHOLASTIC

Scholastic Children's Books
An imprint of Scholastic Ltd
Euston House, 24 Eversholt Street, London, NW1 1DB, UK
Registered office: Westfield Road, Southam, Warwickshire, CV47 0RA
SCHOLASTIC, TOMBQUEST and associated logos are
trademarks and/or registered trademarks of Scholastic Inc.

First published in the US by Scholastic Inc., 2016
First published in the UK by Scholastic Ltd, 2016

ISBN 978 1407 16332 1

A CIP catalogue record for this book
is available from the British Library.

Printed by CPI Group (UK) Ltd, Croydon, CR0 4YY
Papers used by Scholastic Children's Books are made
from wood grown in sustainable forests.

1 3 5 7 9 10 8 6 4 2

www.scholastic.co.uk

For Team TombQuest:
It takes many talented people to make
a book, and even more to get that book to
readers. When it comes to an epic adventure
series like this one, the author is just the tip
of the pyramid, and I am lucky to work
with a team for the ages.

ON THE RUN

Moving at a dead run through an unfamiliar city, Alex Sennefer risked a quick look behind him. Were the guards from the museum still after them? Had the police joined the chase? At first, all he saw was a broad street and wide sidewalks, lit at even intervals by streetlights and dotted with night-time walkers. Then he heard a shout, sharp and clear: *"Halt!"* A guard rounded a corner and came into view, his tie flapping as his shoes slapped the sidewalk.

Is he armed? wondered Alex. *Are there half a*

dozen more men right behind him? He turned to his best friend, Renata Duran, who was running beside him. "We need to get off this" – he huffed in another breath – "street" – puffed it out – "and hide!"

"Yeah!" said Ren. She was twelve years old, like Alex, but small for her age, and her short legs pumped furiously to keep up. "Which way?"

To their left was a large, dark park, a slumbering stretch of trimmed grass and thick trees, surrounded by a tall iron fence. Alex scanned the fence line for an opening but then thought better of it. A fence could protect them – but it could also trap them inside.

Across the street to the right was a long stretch of open sidewalk and closed shops.

"Go right!" Alex said.

"OK," said Ren, "but not yet..."

Alex looked back – now a second guard was running just behind the first.

"Uh, are you sure?" said Alex.

"Wait!" Ren called.

"Why?" he asked. Then he noticed a vague rumbling noise.

"Just keep running!"

Alex swung his head around and saw a single, large headlight in the centre of the street. Steel tracks in the road caught the growing light. It was a streetcar, heading towards them.

"Got it!" he shouted. The two friends sprinted off the sidewalk and into the street, straight towards the oncoming train.

The streetcar sounded its horn: a harsh, electric blare.

The guards were closer now and called out in German again: *"Halt! Vorsicht!"*

But Alex barely heard them as he sprinted across the deadly steel tracks right behind Ren. The horn blared, voices cried out, and the massive car rumbled forward. If he tripped, he'd be cut in half by heavy steel wheels. But with a few quick, careful strides, he and Ren cleared the tracks.

The streetcar rumbled on. Through the windows, Alex could see its few passengers gaping at the brazen duo.

By the time it passed, the two friends were gone. The street was quiet once more, and the guards were bent over, hands on knees, breathing heavily and staring into several small, dark side streets. The trespassers were headed down one of them. They just didn't know which one.

*

"I think we lost them," said Ren as the pair hustled down a short street called Robert Stolz Platz. The street ended in a small park, this one unfenced, and the friends skirted its dark edges.

"Great," said Alex, taking a quick look back and slowing his pace. "Then it's official: We're all lost."

They took a left on to a street bearing the improbable name Nibelungengasse and slowed to a walk. "Yeah," said Ren, breathing heavily and looking both ways down the little street. "Seriously. Where *are* we?"

He knew she didn't mean what street or even what neighbourhood. She meant what city? What country? They had arrived here through a false door, a ceremonial ancient Egyptian portal that had somehow allowed them to travel from the Valley of the Kings in Egypt to another false door in the Egyptian wing of a museum here – wherever *here* was.

For weeks, Alex and Ren had been on the hunt for two things: Alex's mom and the powerful Lost Spells of the Egyptian Book of the Dead. His mom had used those Spells to revive him as he lay on life support in a New York hospital. But in doing so, she'd opened a gateway to the afterlife and the sinister ancient entities known as the Death Walkers had escaped. She and the Spells vanished after that, and Alex and Ren had travelled halfway around the world to find them.

But they weren't the only ones. The Order's deadly operatives were looking for them, too, and hounded the friends wherever they went. They knew the evil cult was working with the Death Walkers in some vast sinister conspiracy. The last Walker had spoken of *ruling* with The Order. Whatever they were up to, it was big, and if the cult found the Spells first, the Death Walkers would be unstoppable, and the whole world would suffer.

Alex shuddered slightly in the night and looked around at a scene that seemed far less grim. The buildings were lit softly by a combination of streetlights and moonlight, and the architecture was old and beautiful. "It's so pretty," said Ren.

"This whole city looks like something you'd find on top of a cake," agreed Alex. He nodded towards a nearby building. It was painted a delicate light green that did, indeed, look a bit like frosting. It reminded him of an exhibit he'd seen at The Metropolitan Museum of Art back in New York, where his mom had worked as an Egyptologist before she disappeared. "Is that, like, art deco?" he said.

Ren shook her head in disapproval. "Don't be ignorant," she said. "It's art nouveau."

"Oh, *obviously*," he said sarcastically, but he didn't doubt her. He was aware that she knew a lot more about it than he did. Her dad was a senior engineer back at the Met, his mom's most trusted coworker, and Ren had inherited his love of elegant angles and solid construction.

"What was that?" Ren gasped, interrupting his thoughts.

"What was what?"

"I thought I saw something slip between those buildings," said Ren, pointing. "Just, like, a shadow."

Alex followed her finger but didn't see anything. "It's the middle of the night," he said. "There are shadows everywhere."

New voices echoed down the little street. A small white dog turned the corner and then two people appeared behind it. "Let's ask them where we are," said Alex.

"Can we trust them?" said Ren.

Alex understood her cautiousness. They had already been betrayed once that night. He could still picture his cousin Luke standing up in the moonlit desert and shouting, *Over here*, giving away their position to the brutal death cult. He was still stunned that his own cousin was working for The Order ... but another glance at the middle-aged couple put his mind at ease. "They've got a shih tzu," he said. "Not exactly an attack dog."

He waved as the couple approached: a man and a woman, wearing casual clothes but fancy shoes. The signs – and shouts – had all been in German so far, but that was the only clue they had about their location. Fortunately, his mom's family was from Germany.

"Hallo!" he called. He knew that part. *"Wo,* um, *sind wir?" Where are we? Maybe?* He was less sure of that, and longed for the smooth, fluid German his mom had always used on the phone with his grandmother.

The man holding the leash smiled and responded with a barrage of rapid-fire German that baffled Alex.

"Ich spreche nur ein bisschen Deutsch," said Alex with an apologetic shrug. *I speak only a little German.*

The woman answered this time, wearing a patient smile and speaking precise English. "You are American, yes? You are on Nibelungengasse."

Ren spoke up. "Not what street," she said. "We'd like to know what city this is."

The dog walkers exchanged quick, confused smiles. Even the dog seemed to regard them with tongue-lolling pity.

"You are in Wien, of course," said the man. "Vienna. Is there something you need help with? Are you . . . lost?"

"No, we're fine," said Alex. "But thanks."

The dog walkers went on their way, but the strangest thing happened as Alex turned to give one last embarrassed wave. He thought he saw a shadow, too, a thin slice of night slipping from one side of the streetlight's glow to the other.

"Wow, Vienna," said Ren, looking around with fresh eyes.

"That's got to be two thousand miles from where we were," said Alex. "And it felt like it took a minute." He remembered their desperate sprint through a strange and murky landscape. . . *Had they really travelled through the afterlife?*

His mind was full of big questions and confusing new realities, but right now he had a more immediate concern. As his eyes scanned the dark edges of the street, he felt the ancient scarab amulet at his neck growing warm against his skin. A warning: Death was lurking nearby.

"Maybe we should, uh, find someplace to stay," he said.

He suddenly wanted to be anywhere other than the dark streets of an unfamiliar city. He reached into the pocket of his jeans, but all he pulled out was a handful of Egyptian bills. Useless. What good was Egyptian capital in the capital of Austria?

"Maybe we can find somewhere to change those when the stores open tomorrow," said Ren.

"Maybe tomorrow," Alex repeated absently. His eyes were fixed on a dark corner that seemed, somehow, to be darker than the rest.

It was tonight he was worried about.

SHADOW OF A DOUBT

A little while later, they found themselves hiding in a secluded park. Around them, as night settled in, the city's lights blinked out one by one.

"I wish we had our tents," said Alex, trying to find a way to sit that didn't involve getting stabbed by tree roots. The park was nice and clean and leafy – as everything in Vienna seemed to be – but it was still a dark and open space. And Alex had other concerns. Shadows shifted all around them, with every gust of wind through the trees.

"Well, the tents are back in Egypt," said Ren matter-of-factly. "All we have is this." She swung her small backpack on to the thick grass and began pawing through it. She pulled out her flashlight and clicked it on and off quickly. "Still works!"

Alex unzipped his backpack, too. He pushed his hand inside and felt around for his flashlight. He felt the burned shirt he'd changed out of, the smooth cover of his passport, and then a little pool of sand that had settled at the bottom of the pack. "Can you believe we were just in the desert?" he said as his hand finally closed around his flashlight.

"I kind of can't believe any of it," said Ren. "We basically ran through a fake door painted on solid stone in Egypt and straight out another one in Austria. And I know the only thing that makes sense is that we travelled through the afterlife – I mean, I saw it. But I still can't believe it. It creeps me out."

Alex was listening, but also looking out into the night. As he did, he saw it again. The darkness seemed to coalesce into a slice of deeper black. Alex pointed his flashlight and clicked it on. But the light cut straight through and hit the trunk of one of the two thick trees they were camped between.

"What are you doing?" said Ren.

"Nothing. I guess I'm just freaked out, too."

Ren looked at him carefully. Her face was a grey oval in the night. "Do you think we're OK?" she said. "I mean, if we travelled through the afterlife ... were we – are we – um, dead?"

Alex shook his head. "I don't think so. I think we were just, like, passing through? It must be the amulets that let us do that." He glanced over at her Egyptian ibis amulet, the image of a pale white bird, glowing faintly in the moonlight. He felt the weight of the scarab hanging from his neck.

"Well, I guess you would know," said Ren, before quickly adding: "I mean because you've had your amulet for longer. Not because. . ."

Alex nodded. He knew what she meant: Not because he'd been dead before.

Not because his mom had accidentally unleashed death so that he could live.

His mom.

The thought hit him like an avalanche: a cold and massive weight. They'd picked up her trail in the Valley of the Kings. They'd been so close to her – and now, just hours later, they were a continent away. It felt frustrating and unfair. He didn't know why she was running. She had always looked after him, always known what to do, so why abandon him now? He couldn't figure it out. But he knew he needed to find her. And not just to put his growing doubts to rest, but also because the Spells she had with her were the only things powerful enough to end the evil spreading across the globe.

A memory flashed through his mind: his mom's handwriting in a government logbook in the Valley of the Kings. She'd signed a fake name, but a familiar one: Angela Felini, one of his old babysitters. But there was no one looking after him now, not his mom and not Angela, who'd moved to Alexandria, Virginia, years ago. Now he felt like he alone was responsible – for himself, and for all the trouble he'd caused.

Ren interrupted his thoughts. "We should call Todtman."

Dr Ernst Todtman was the leader of their unlikely group, and the last time they'd seen him was in Cairo. They hadn't heard from the mysterious German scholar since they'd split up to cover more ground.

"Yeah, definitely," said Alex. He dug into his pocket for his disposable cell phone – what Ren called his "spy phone." He clicked it on and checked the screen. He'd had calls from his own phone forwarded to it – just in case his mom tried to reach him – but he had no missed calls at all. And now the battery was almost dead.

"Do you think our phones will work here?"

"Maybe. They worked in London and Egypt. Todtman must have got, like, the international plan when he bought the phones."

Alex dialled, but once again the call went straight to voice mail. He left a quick message.

"It's me. We're in Vienna. Austria. I'll try to explain when you call us. A lot has happened. Don't trust Luke. Please call!"

Ren ruined some of the urgency of Alex's message by letting out a mighty yawn. "Sorry," she said. "Really tired."

"Me too," said Alex. "I guess we should get some sleep and try Todtman again in the morning."

"What if they find us?"

They. Alex knew she didn't mean the guards from the museum. She meant The Order. "We left them in the dust back in Egypt," he said, hoping it was true. "Or the sand, anyway. There's no way they could know we ended up here."

"OK," Ren said sleepily. She put her backpack behind her head and lay down on the soft grass. "Maybe one of us should stay awake and keep watch."

"I'll take the first watch," said Alex. He was really tired but felt like he owed it to her. He was the reason she was here in the first place.

Ren fell asleep immediately, leaving Alex alone with his thoughts. He leaned against his backpack and gazed into the dark summer night. The air was warm and the faintest strains of classical music floated out from some open window far away. He scanned the shadows, measured the darkness. He told himself there was nothing there – but he didn't quite believe it. He needed to know for sure.

He reached up and slipped the ancient scarab amulet from under his shirt. It was plain and chunky as Egyptian artefacts went, just polished stone and refined copper. But the scarab beetle was a powerful symbol of resurrection in ancient Egypt, and the amulet had tremendous power. It could activate the Book of the Dead and banish the Death Walkers; it could move objects and summon powerful winds; and lastly, it could detect the undead.

Alex closed his hand around it. Even as his pulse revved with ancient energy, he sought to calm his mind. To open up and stretch out with his senses... For a second, he thought he felt something: a slight presence no more substantial than the last soap bubble in the sink. But then it slipped away. It was such a weak signal that he wasn't entirely sure he had felt it at all.

He released the amulet and chastised himself. He had too much real trouble to go inventing more. A Death Walker would light up his amulet like a battleship on a radar screen. Why drive himself crazy with a weak, slippery signal that might not exist at all?

It had been a long day with lots of running. Alex's grimy nylon backpack wasn't much of a pillow, but he was sure he could lie back and relax a little and still stay awake. But a moment later, his eyes fluttered closed, and he fell fast asleep.

The shadow had followed them from the afterlife. It liked this new boy who was shadowed by death, too. How was it possible to bear the marks of death and still be so full of life? The shadow didn't know, but it wondered if it could take that energy for itself.

If it could gorge on this boy's life and become full. Maybe it would even remember who it had been, once upon a time, so long ago.

It leaned over Alex as he slept, and pinched his nose shut.

Alex immediately began to squirm. It was a soft movement at first, as if rolling to get more comfortable. But as the oxygen ceased to flow, he twisted with a bit more urgency.

The shadow concentrated. At first it was all it could do to hold the nostrils of the squirming boy closed. It was still a weak presence in this world, and this was the outer limit of its influence here.

Alex opened his mouth and gasped. That was what the shadow had been waiting for. The strange creature breathed deeply, sucking the warm air leaving Alex's lungs straight into its own dark form. And as it did, it grew stronger. Its hand grew more defined. What had been little more than a cold, dark paw now resolved itself into individual fingers, a wrist.

The shadow pressed its new hand down over Alex's nose. He thrashed beneath the increasing force and, finally, his eyes snapped open.

What he saw made no sense to him, just an

impenetrable darkness hanging over him. And then he saw its milky grey eyes.

It was a sheut, the shadowy vessel that the ancient Egyptians believed contained a person's spirit and self, their ka and ba. Alex had seen the pooled blackness at the feet of the living in the ancient art at the Met. But the body of this one was long dead, and the ka and ba had fled. Something had gone wrong, and they hadn't been reunited in the afterlife. All that was left was this thing of darkness: a shadow of its former self.

Alex watched in horror as a stream of soft white fog rose from his own open mouth and disappeared into the sheut. He rolled and thrashed, but the hand pressed down hard. *How can a shadow hold me?* Alex wondered desperately. But hold him it did. Stronger with each breath it stole, it pinned his head hard against the ground. *It is taking my strength*, Alex suddenly realized. *It is taking my life force as its own!*

Alex reached up to wrestle the thing away, but his hands passed straight through the apparition's arms. It could affect him, but he couldn't affect it.

His amulet!

Alex's lungs cried out for oxygen even as they gave it up. He felt his vision narrowing. He was on the verge of passing out. He reached desperately for his amulet and found only its silver chain. The heavy scarab had swung around behind him as he slept and was now pinned between the back of his neck and the ground.

As its grey eyes turned milky white, the sheut lowered them towards Alex. *How isss it you arrre allllliiiive?* it asked, the words taking shape not on the air but inside Alex's mind. He had no breath left to answer. And it didn't seem to matter: He wouldn't be alive for long.

THE MOON IN HER HAND

Under the stars and between the trees a few feet away, Ren was sound asleep and dreaming of home. Since this mission had started, she'd travelled around the world to battle Death Walkers and search for the Lost Spells and Alex's mom. And along the way, her homesickness had progressed to something like home flu. Sleep was her only chance to visit.

Her mom and dad were at the table in the small kitchen of their New York City apartment. Ren could tell immediately that it was a workday.

Her mom was dressed in a sharp jacket and pencil skirt combo, set for another day of high-powered public relations work. She didn't yet know which of the company's clients had said or done something stupid, but she was prepared for anything. Her dad was in one of his familiar button-down shirts, the sleeves already rolled, the mechanical pencil in the chest pocket. Ready to solve problems of a more precise variety.

They talked softly over the last of their coffee, slipping into Spanish now and then as they sometimes did. Ren understood every word this time. That wasn't always the case at home, but she was dreaming these words, after all. As she slept, a tear slipped through the corner of one closed eye. They were talking about her.

They were wondering how she was doing in London. They were proud of her internship at the British Museum. They missed her.

I miss you, too, Ren wanted to say. The rest of it she wouldn't mention, because she was a long way from London now – a long way from a fake internship. But it didn't matter. She had no voice in this dream.

The phone began to ring. Her father stood up. But

something was wrong. He walked over to the sink and dumped out the dregs of his coffee, ignoring the phone entirely. And that ring – or tone, rather – flat and electronic. Generic, like. . .

A disposable cell phone.

Ren's eyes drifted open.

She reached up to wipe the tear away with one hand and reached down for her phone with the other. But her phone was quiet and still. "Alex," she said, turning towards her friend. "Your phone."

And that's when she saw it. Alex was flopping limply, like a fish too long on the dock, and a dark shape was looming over him. A human shape. Weak light filtered into the park from the streetlamps at its margins and the moon above, and it all ended at the edges of this entity. Its hand was clamped down over Alex's face, and a thin vaporous line ran from his open mouth to the creature's. Right away, Ren knew it was killing him.

"Stop it!" she screamed.

The sheut turned and regarded her with softly glowing eyes. It was strong now, unthreatened.

Ren balled up her fists. She was small for her age, but brave for anyone's. This thing was terrifying and she felt her own chest tighten with fear, but she was not going to let it take her friend. She. Was. Not. She needed to knock it loose, to allow him to breathe. She took a deep breath – and leapt at it!

She passed straight through, feeling nothing but a profound chill, and crashed to the ground on the other side. She looked back, baffled and desperate. The line of vapor was almost gone now. She got up and swung at it with her fists.

Nothing. It felt like dipping them in cold milk but had no effect at all.

Think, she told herself. *Be smart.*

My amulet.

She reached up. The ibis was a symbol of Thoth, the ancient Egyptian god of wisdom, writing and moonlight, and its main power was to show her images and provide information. She'd grown a little more comfortable with it lately, but she still distrusted the magic behind it. It just felt weird having it in her head like that – like letting a wild horse into a quiet study hall. But now she needed that power. She needed that wild horse – for once, she didn't even care if she could rein it in.

Her hand closed around the ibis. This time she asked it not for answers, but for justice. Thoth was the one who wrote down the verdict at the weighing

23

of the heart ceremony, the test to determine whether a soul gained entrance into the afterlife. He was the divine scribe, the one who made sure everything was in the right place, written in the right column. Ren liked things in their right place, too, and she knew for a fact that this deathly presence did not belong here.

She squeezed the ibis tight, feeling its edges dig into her palm.

"Go!" she shouted. And as she did, a burst of blinding white light flashed outward, like the full moon pressed down to the size of one small, fierce fist and then released again.

The sheut hissed against the light and was torn to shreds, like a cheap black suit caught up in a hurricane.

When the light faded, it was gone.

Alex gasped for breath.

His phone beeped once. Voice mail.

The sheut had popped like a black balloon in the moonlight. Now, a few last wisps of Alex's breath hung over him like a pale white cloud in the warm night. *So that's it*, he thought, looking up at the slowly scattering vapor. *That's what all this is about.* It was more than breath, he knew; it was life.

How can this little cloud of breath be worth so much trouble? he wondered as the last gasp dissolved. *How can I be worth so much trouble? Ren saved me this time, but how many others have died because I lived? How many more will die before we can find the Spells and end all of this? If we even can. The doorway to the afterlife seems to open wider every day. All because of me. . .*

Ren knelt down by his side. "How do you feel?" she asked.

Alex forced a smile. "Awful," he said. It was a familiar feeling and one he'd hoped he'd never feel again. There were painful pinpricks in his arms and legs, fingers and toes, as if he'd just come in from too long in the cold. He felt tired and nauseous. He'd felt this way nearly his whole life, before the Spells had transformed him. He looked up at Ren. "I feel like before."

"Oh no," she said. Apart from his mom, Ren was the one person who knew just how bad "before" had been. She shook off her concerned expression and forced a smile of her own. "You just need to recover your strength."

Alex nodded and sat there breathing and rubbing his arms. The more he breathed, the better he felt.

Finally, Alex reached for his phone to check the missed call. Now he smiled for real.

"Todtman?" said Ren hopefully.

Alex gave her a big thumbs-up and put the phone on speaker so Ren could hear the message, too.

"Hello, Alex. I got your message. I am sorry for the ... delay. I am glad to hear from you." Alex leaned closer to the phone. He was glad to hear the crisp consonants of Todtman's familiar German accent again, but his voice was obscured by a faint buzzing. "Things have got worse in Cairo. The voices of the dead are everywhere now; the city is in chaos. I had to leave. I can be in Vienna by tomorrow, mid-morning. There is a small restaurant on Linke Wienzeile, near the Naschmarkt." As he rattled off the address, Alex heard Ren rustling around for her ever-present pen. "I will meet you there at ten thirty. Stay safe."

They played the message again with the last of the battery power, just to make sure they had the address right.

"I am going to eat *so* much at that restaurant," said Ren.

But Alex didn't want to talk about Wiener schnitzel. He pictured the terrible darkness that had loomed over him just minutes earlier. "Thanks," he said. "You saved my life."

"Saved your life *again*. But," Ren added, "I have no idea how."

"You banished it," Alex said, "with the light from your amulet."

Ren considered that. "I just knew that thing didn't belong here," she said. "And you're welcome."

Alex didn't get much sleep for the rest of the night. Instead, he kept watch. He was sure the sheut had followed them from the afterlife. *What if something else had?*

And there was another shadow that wasn't so easy to dismiss. This one wasn't looming over him, but lurking inside. Ren's words played on a loop in his head: *That thing didn't belong here*, she'd said. And she was right. It had returned from the afterlife, after all.

But then, hadn't Alex done the same thing when his mom brought him back?

He watched the new day dawn in softly glowing purples and pinks and wondered: *Do I have any more right to this sunrise than that desperate spirit did?*

BOXED IN

They arrived at the restaurant a few minutes early. "Schnitzel Box," said Ren, reading the sign. "Promising."

Alex heard his stomach rumble in agreement. He'd recovered his health, and with it, his appetite.

"How do you say *large* in German?" asked Ren.

"*Gross*," said Alex.

"Seriously?"

He nodded.

"Well, I am going to have the grossest schnitzel

28

they've got," said Ren. "Let's go on in and wait for Todtman inside. They won't mind."

"We don't have enough money for a place like this," said Alex.

"We can just drink a bunch of water until Todtman gets here," said Ren. "And use the bathroom."

They pushed through the door into the restaurant's dimly lit, dark wood interior. The place was dead.

"Welcome," said the lone waiter, a tall man in a white shirt and black vest. "Sit anywhere you would like. We have just opened."

Alex was surprised to hear the man greet them in English. Was it that obvious they were Americans? *"Danke!"* he said. "Thanks."

He headed straight for the restrooms, looked for the picture with pants, and went in that door. After taking care of some pressing business, he headed to the sink. He felt like a mess after a night in the park and another near-death experience, and let the water run until it was nice and hot.

After scrubbing his hands, he swished some water around in his mouth. His own dirt-smudged face stared back at him from the mirror as he ran one wet hand through his mussed-up black hair.

His fingers caught halfway and he winced. He'd need to get some shampoo in there one of these days. There'd be time for that later. He felt a buzz of anticipation. Soon they'd see Todtman, have a big meal and resume their search for his mom and the Spells.

Finally, he bent down and splashed hot water on his face. He dipped his hands in the sink again as he straightened up and checked the mirror to see if he'd removed at least some of the dirt. But he barely saw his face at all, because the face behind it was so much more terrifying.

Looking straight at him was a man with the head of a giant housefly. On either side were large eyes the size of half grapefruits and made up of thousands of individual lenses. Alex's body froze from fear, but his mind raced. A mask in the shape of an animal head told him this man was an operative of The Order.

They'd found him.

He whirled around, splashing hot water on the tile floor as his hand reached desperately for the scarab. The thousand-eyed gaze followed him, the eyes of the mask shifting and moving as if alive. Painful experience had taught him that the masks were as ancient and powerful as his own amulet.

A strong hand grabbed Alex's left wrist before he could reach the chain at his neck. He reached up with his right, only to have that pinned, too. He struggled, trying to free his wrists, water still dripping from his hands. The fly head leaned in and regarded him with its bulbous eyes, and an overwhelming stink of garbage made Alex gag. A crashing sound reached his ears as furniture was overturned and silverware clattered to the floor out in the restaurant.

Ren. He'd led her into trouble – again.

Desperate, he struggled harder. It was useless. The fly man held him tight with hairy gnarled hands and regarded Alex with the eight thousand shifting lenses of his composite eyes. Then the fly man spoke: "Hello, Alex. I got your message. I am sorry for the . . . delay."

His voice was a perfect imitation of Todtman's, though it was true, there was a slight buzz to it. The phone call, the meeting – it had all been a trap! Alex needed to act now to have any chance of escape. There was another crash from the restaurant and a high-pitched yelp. *Was Ren hurt?*

Alex kicked out hard. The toe of his boot sank into the thick folds of the fly's grimy robe and clipped the knobby leg underneath. His attacker flinched slightly, but instead of releasing him, his grip grew tighter. Alex kicked again. He was wearing good boots, designed for the desert, and this time, he caught the fly flush on the shin. The fly doubled over, releasing his grip and coughing out a cloud of disgusting brownish green gas.

Alex held his breath – and grabbed his amulet with his left hand. Wet palm against cold stone, he formed the now-familiar words in his mind: *The wind that comes before the rain.* The scarab was a symbol of rebirth in Egypt, and this was among its most powerful manifestations. His right hand shot forward and with it an invisible lance of rushing wind.

The fly-headed operative took the blast directly in the gut. The wind was strong – and the floor was wet. His sandalled feet skated straight back.

WAMMP! He hit the wall hard.

Alex bolted out the door. In the dining room, Alex was relieved not to see a squad of Order gunmen. Instead, he saw the waiter holding a large carving knife and chasing Ren around an overturned table.

"Hey!" shouted Alex.

The waiter turned towards Alex. He might as

well have stepped into a wind tunnel. He tumbled over the upturned table and landed amid crashes and clinks on the other side. *"Autsch, eine Gabel!"* he cried. *Ow, a fork!*

The door to the men's room flew open and a fetid stink seeped into the chase-wrecked room, but as it did, the front door flew open as well. The two friends rushed out into daylight – and fresh air.

The friends took twenty blocks' worth of twists and turns at a dead run, stopping only when they were sure – well, pretty sure – that they'd given the world's largest fly and rudest waiter the slip. At the end of it, they'd found a public bench and another voice mail from Todtman, this one on Ren's phone.

"How do we know it's really him this time?" she huffed.

"Look at the time: 10:28 a.m.," said Alex, pointing down at the screen of Ren's phone. "It has to be Todtman. That's when the fly guy was busy attacking me. Remember? We got there a little early."

Alex took another look at the screen, this time eyeing the little sliver of remaining battery life. "Play the message again," he said.

She did. And then, looking both ways and huddling close together on the little bench, they called the new number he'd given them. Todtman answered immediately. Ren put it on speaker and Alex listened carefully to his voice, but this time there was no buzziness as they got down to business.

They gave Todtman a quick recap, including Luke's betrayal and their current location, so that he could send someone to pick up the two remaining friends. Alex knew that Todtman was well-connected and never seemed to be short of cash. Still, he was surprised when a snow-white limo pulled up to the kerb in front of them half an hour later. Somewhat sceptically, he asked the driver for the password.

The man was wearing a black suit and a Bluetooth earpiece. "Tutankhamun," he said flatly as he walked around the car to open the back door for them.

Ren nodded – she had chosen it – and they both climbed in and headed to the airport, where their plane tickets back to Egypt were waiting.

"No offence," she said as the long car snaked through midday traffic, "but was this, like, the last car left?"

The driver gave her a half look over his shoulder.

"Not at all," he said. "Your uncle requested this one in particular."

Alex and Ren exchanged looks, and Ren silently mouthed two words: *Our uncle?*

Alex had heard worse cover stories. "Why?" he said.

The driver shrugged. "Because the airports are being watched, and no one will expect you to pull up in a white limousine." He glanced in the mirror and must have caught the surprised expressions of his passengers, because he added: "I am a professional. Now relax and enjoy the trip."

"But what if—" began Ren.

Alex cut her off: "Don't mind my *little* sister," he called up to the driver. And then, more softly: "You probably can't see her over the seat, anyway."

Ren gave him a good-natured punch in the arm. Good-natured – but not exactly soft.

In an hour and a half, they were on a small plane. Three and a half hours and fourteen tiny bags of free pretzels later, they touched down at a small, regional airport thirty-five miles outside of Cairo. Todtman met them as they were headed for customs, which was, of course, against all the rules.

"How did you get past security?" said Alex. He

tried to keep his tone as businesslike as Todtman's, but he couldn't help smiling at the sight of the old German alive and well, with his froglike bulging eyes and trademark black suit. "Did you bribe them or hypnotize them with your amulet?" He glanced at the jewel-eyed falcon at Todtman's neck.

"Why can't it be both?" Todtman whispered with a sly smile of his own.

The customs official waved them through, not even pretending to look at their passports. The trio exited into the brightly lit expanse of the terminal.

"We must hurry," said Todtman, the rubber tip of his jet-black walking stick plunking the tile and his eyes sweeping the terminal. "We are not safe here."

"In this airport?" said Ren, looking around warily.

"In Egypt," said Todtman.

READING THE SIGNS

Driving a large, beat-up rental car, Todtman took off from the airport with only slightly less velocity than the jets roaring by above. Stuck in the back seat, Alex fastened his seat belt tightly. Ren had called shotgun before it had even occurred to him, claiming the front seat with a triumphant chirp: "Revenge of the 'little sister'."

Todtman shifted to coax more power out of the big engine, but the gears caught and the car lurched alarmingly. "Sorry," he said. "There were no German cars available."

A turn came up, and Todtman took it. Another one appeared, and he took that one, too. Soon, there was more traffic, and the low smudge of a small city appeared on the horizon. Todtman downshifted, slowed. Alex relaxed. They'd slipped free from the airport into the teeming mix of a country of nearly ninety million.

They skirted around the little city, avoiding narrow streets and slow traffic, and stuck to a wide road surrounded by surprisingly green country. A battered old tractor appeared up ahead, and Todtman switched lanes and left it in the dust.

"Why'd you pick us up out here in the boondocks?" asked Ren.

"Cairo is too dangerous," said Todtman. "The spirits have driven too many to madness; the authorities are overwhelmed – and The Order does as it pleases."

Alex peered out the back window, remembering the chaos he'd witnessed in Cairo: the shouts and sirens, the people haunted by voices in their heads, the woman who ran headlong through a shop window, the police huddled together for their own protection, The Order thugs carrying their guns openly... "So it's even worse now?" he said, trying to imagine it.

"Much worse," said Todtman. He caught Alex's eyes in the rearview mirror. "I barely escaped with my life – or my soul." He fell silent for a few moments, as if fighting back a painful memory.

Alex broke eye contact. He felt like he was riding in the back of a police car: *guilty*. Cairo was lost, all of Egypt was unsafe, the madness spread farther every day ... and he was the cause of it all.

"So it's more important than ever that we find my mom and the Lost Spells," he said, trying to keep things on track. "Have you found out any more about where she might be?"

Todtman shook his head. "Nothing."

"So which way are we headed, then?" Alex demanded. He looked out the tinted window and saw a green field. Two skinny black cows stood grazing on ankle-high grass, while acres of deeper green leaves stretched out behind them. They were in the Nile delta, north of Cairo, a land of dark, fertile soil.

"That is what we must determine," Todtman answered. "Our next destination, the next step."

"We know Alex's mom was in the Valley of the Kings," offered Ren. "But that was more than a week ago."

"And now The Order will know she was there, too," said Alex glumly. "Because Luke was spying for them the whole time."

Alex had been betrayed by his cousin and abandoned by his mom. It was a powerful one-two punch, and once again he felt the impact. He shook his head hard, trying to refocus. "Yeah, she'll be far away from the Valley by now," he concluded.

Todtman nodded and then added: "The thing that makes finding your mother so hard is..." He paused. Alex leaned forward in anticipation of some difficult admission, some new truth about his mom. But when it came, the truth was more about Todtman. "She is smarter than I am. She always was – just a little."

Despite the clouds hanging over his thoughts, a small smile slipped on to Alex's face.

"That's OK," said Ren. "She's smarter than Alex, too."

The smile slipped right back off.

They zoomed by more fields, the stalks of golden wheat on one small farm giving way to a grove of short, squat banana trees on the next. Shallow irrigation ditches divided the landscape. Todtman downshifted as they slipped on to a side road, kicking up a dusty plume behind them. "We will need to think carefully, to figure out what Maggie is trying to do," he said. "We must think back over everything we've found – see if there are any clues we missed."

Alex hesitated, but there was one thing he'd kept circling back to. "I don't know if it means anything," he began, "but the name my mom signed in the logbook when she left the Valley of the Kings, Angela Felini..."

Ren leaned across the front seat towards Todtman. "Angie was his old babysitter," she said, in that teacher's pet way she sometimes fell into.

"Yeah," said Alex. "It's just ... after she stopped working for us she moved to Alexandria. I mean, Alexandria, Virginia, but still. Do you think that my mom signed that name as, like, a message? To me? To us? Because I know there's an Alexandria, *Egypt*, too."

"Hmmmm," said Todtman. "It seems possible. If she anticipated us following her..."

"Well, she is smarter than us," said Alex. He wanted desperately to believe it: that even if his

41

mom had deserted him, she hadn't forgotten him. If she'd left him a clue, it could mean that she was still looking out for him. That she wasn't completely abandoning him.

"She talked about Alexandria sometimes," he added hopefully.

"Yeah, because she went to school there," said Ren.

Had she really? Alex tried to remember. When he thought of his mom in school, he thought of Columbia, in New York City. That was the sweatshirt she wore, the campus they visited for alumni events sometimes. He knew she'd got her PhD in Egypt, though. He tried to remember exactly where, but Ren was still one step ahead of him.

"There's a degree on the wall of your place," she said. "By the bookshelf."

"Oh yeah," said Alex. He had a vague memory of a framed sheet of old vellum on the wall of the little apartment where he'd grown up. He'd seen it so many times that he'd almost stopped seeing it. He tried to remember the big words at the top. It was a degree, had to be, the writing in Arabic and English. He closed his eyes . . . *Alexandria University.*

"You're right," he said, looking up towards the

front seat, but the little grin on Ren's face told him she already knew that. *Leave it to Ren to notice all the degrees on the wall*, he thought. Still, it was a little awkward for his best friend to remember something about his mom that he hadn't. "You're not *really* my sister, you know," he added.

Ren opened her mouth to reply, but Todtman cut in.

"Yes, that's right," he said, his froggy face bending upward in a smile of his own. "I knew she finished her dissertation in Egypt. But I assumed it was in Cairo. Alexandria University is an old school, and a good one."

"That's why she still talks about Alexandria," said Alex. "It was the first place she lived in Egypt."

"Yes," said Todtman, "her roots in this country are in Alexandria. And if I'm not mistaken, yours, too, Alex."

"What do you mean?" he said. She definitely hadn't told him that.

"What is your name?"

"It's Alex – oh!" He slumped down in his seat, his head reeling from the implications. *Alex ... Alexandria.* "Wasn't Alexandria named after Alexander the Great?" he said.

Todtman nodded, and Ren snorted, clearly unconvinced of her best friend's Greatness. Alex didn't notice. He was staring down at his own legs. His own Egyptian legs.

"That university is her oldest and deepest connection to this country," said Todtman, taking the next left with the car, pointing them back towards the main road. "So that is where the trail points us."

A buzzing line of fast-moving cars appeared up ahead. A highway. Alex scanned a tall blue sign near the entrance. Various destinations were listed in Arabic and English in reflective white paint. His eyes ran to the third line:

ALEXANDRIA 153 KILOMETRES

"Look, Alex," said Ren, turning around in her seat to face him. "You're going home!"

Ren glanced to her side and saw Todtman's eyes staring straight at the road ahead, his hands precisely at ten and two o'clock on the steering wheel. She looked into the mirror and saw Alex lost in thought in the back seat.

They had their destination, but the clue leading them there felt like a long shot. She wanted to know if they were headed in the right direction – or off on another Egyptian goose chase. Slowly, silently, she peeled her hand from the cool vinyl of the car seat and reached up for her amulet.

She'd never done this before. She'd never asked the ibis for answers without being forced to – without a Death Walker looming or Todtman insisting. But maybe she could try now, she thought. Maybe if she just kept it to herself, she wouldn't feel the same pressure to get it exactly right.

Ren took a deep, nervous breath. She exhaled softly and whispered two words: "Extra credit." They were powerful words for the girl known as "Plus Ten Ren" back in school. She had always had a bad habit of putting too much pressure on herself on tests and assignments, and sometimes it cost her. But she gobbled up every bit of available extra credit, work that could only help, never hurt. And back in the Valley of the Kings, that approach – viewing her amulet's mysterious offerings as a bonus – had helped her get a handle on its magic, as well.

As her hand closed around it, she once again asked for a little extra. She felt the smooth stone against her palm and, a split second later, a sudden jolt of energy. Her eyes closed and her mind filled with images:

A baby with fat, tan cheeks and wide brown eyes,

staring out at a massive container ship gliding slowly across smooth, dark water. . .

A young woman's hand, reaching down to pick up a stack of thick books, a rubber band around her wrist – a rubber band just like Alex's mom used to wear sometimes. . .

Her eyes opened.

"What did you see?" said Todtman.

She looked over at him, blinking twice to refocus her eyes back in the here and now. "Is Alexandria on the coast?" she asked.

"Yes, the Mediterranean," said Todtman. "It has been Egypt's main port for centuries."

"What are you two talking about?" chirped Alex from the back seat.

"Nothing," said Ren, catching his eyes in the mirror. His cheeks weren't quite so chubby any more, but she was pretty sure his was the face she'd seen. And that must have been his mom's arms, picking up her schoolbooks. And if all that was true, then that seaside city was Alexandria.

"Is there something we should know?" said Todtman, eyeing her ibis.

Ren shook her head. "No, we're good," she said. "Just keep driving."

Their destination no longer felt like such a long shot to her, but there were still a lot of *ifs* and *maybes* in those images. And the only thing she hated more than being unsure was being wrong. She'd used her amulet voluntarily, and it hadn't been so bad. But it had tricked her before – and she knew there were much tougher tests ahead.

ALEXANDRIA

They drove through the evening and approached Alexandria in the dead of night. Alex felt a little spike of hope as he saw the modest skyline take murky shape in the moonlight. Maybe his mom's past really was the key to her present. It made sense. *In a vast, foreign country, wouldn't she stick to the places she knew?* He hoped they'd find another clue – or better yet, his mom herself.

But Alex was worried, too. The closer they got, the more the questions dogged him: *Why was she running? Why didn't she contact him?* A scary thought popped into his head, fully formed: *She's given me life twice now – is she angry about what it has cost?* He shook his head hard to clear it. He felt frustrated and guilty and lost as his thoughts slid by darkly, like the view outside the car windows. *I need to make this right. It's up to me.* This time his head stayed as still as stone.

Alexandria was a city of millions, and the houses on the outskirts quickly gave way to bigger buildings: apartments, offices, stores. But most of them were dark now, lumbering shadows slipping silently by. Only streetlights and sparse headlights lit their way.

"I have an old colleague that we can stay with," said Todtman. "We'll be safe there while we follow your mom's trail."

Alex leaned forward to assess their surroundings. The neighbourhood had changed again. The big blocky buildings had given way to smaller, sleeker ones. Shiny metal edges and wide glass windows caught the headlights as they passed, the subtle flourishes of expensive modern architecture. "Uh, these are really fancy houses," said Alex.

"This is like the Upper East Side of Alexandria," said Ren, and Alex laughed despite himself.

"How do you say *Park Avenue* in Arabic?" he said.

Ren chortled. "Is this guy rich?" she asked Todtman, leaning forward for a better look.

"This *woman*," said Todtman. "And very."

Todtman pulled into a driveway and stopped at a metal gate. He lowered his window and said something into a speaker in rapid, hushed Arabic. A few moments later, the gate slid back with a smooth mechanical hum.

There was a conspicuously expensive car in the driveway in front of them, and the gate slid shut behind them with a firm, precise *SHUUNK*. Alex looked up at the ultramodern cube of a house. A ring of outside lights had come on, and a few of the inside ones were now visible behind large squares of blue-tinted glass on the second floor. "What does this lady do, exactly?" he said.

"She is" – Todtman pursed his lips, considering his word choice – "a collector... Yes, a bit of a scholar, certainly, but only in a private capacity. Mostly she ... collects."

Alex didn't like all those pauses one bit. He knew that private collections of Egyptian artefacts were put together on the black market as often as at the auction house. "And how do you know her, again?"

Todtman flashed him half a smile, but in the dim light of the car's interior, Alex couldn't tell if it meant "trust me" or "you don't want to know". He looked up at the house again and saw a shadow glide silently across one window.

The door clicked open as they approached it, and Alex gawped at the little fish-eyed camera lens as they passed. They entered the hushed, half-lit entryway and were met by a large, imposing man – who imposed himself immediately.

"Wait here," he said gruffly, but his expression changed when he saw Todtman's face. "Oh, hey, Doc. Just a minute."

Alex sized up the man – extra-large – and guessed he was a live-in security guard.

"It's all right, Bubbi," called a woman's voice from somewhere in the shadowy house. "I'm in the study, Doctor!"

The big man stepped aside, and Alex wondered if his bodyguard buddies knew he was called Bubbi. Todtman led the way up a flight of stairs and into a broad and brightly lit room. A woman approached them dressed in business attire despite the hour: tapered tan slacks and

51

a crisp white blouse. She was about his mom's age, he figured, and carried herself in a similarly professional manner.

She greeted Todtman warmly and then turned to Alex and Ren.

"My name is Safa," she said. "You are welcome in my home."

Alex felt tense. He didn't know anything about this woman, and here they were boxing themselves up inside a walled compound with her. He'd planned to say something polite but measured, like "Hello" or "Thanks for letting us crash". Instead, he found himself gawking wordlessly at the room around him. Ancient stone relief carvings lined the walls; a life-sized statue stood in a lit alcove.

"Are these all Hatshepsut?" he blurted finally.

Safa's measured expression broke into a warm smile. "Yes, the world's finest private collection," she said, the pride unmistakable in her voice.

Alex took another quick look at the array of ancient artwork, all showing Egypt's first female pharaoh. "Wow. Wasn't most of her stuff destroyed?" he said. The Met had an entire room of carvings of Hatshepsut, but those pieces had been reconstructed.

"I see the apple doesn't fall far from the tree," said Safa. "But look closer."

Alex took a few steps towards the statue, and now he saw it. The same light lines in the stone that the ones at the Met had, the subtle scars of expert reconstruction. And what he had initially thought was a heavy shadow on one side of the face was, in fact, all that was left of the face. One side had been chipped away, and there was a patch of rough grey stone where the left eye and cheek should have been. Her chin ended not in the symbolic beard of a pharaoh, but in chisel marks.

"This one is all in one piece," said Ren, pointing to an elegant relief along the wall that showed the sleek, regal figure of Hatshepsut standing on one side of a bearded pharaoh as the falcon-headed sun god, Amun-Re, stood on the other.

"Good eye, child," said Safa, turning. "Images of Hatshepsut as queen were left untouched. It was only the ones that showed her as ruler in her own right that were destroyed. The next pharaoh wanted to make sure it was his descendants and not hers who would take the throne."

"So unfair," said Ren.

"The world has always been a difficult place for

powerful women," said Safa with a somewhat weary smile. "I keep these here as both a tribute and a reminder."

As she began walking out of the room, Alex remembered what he'd meant to say in the first place. "Thank you for letting us stay here," he said. "It helps a lot."

"And I am happy to help," said Safa, still walking. For a moment, it seemed like that would be all, but a few steps later, she stopped and turned to face him.

"You know, it was your mother who first led me to Hatshepsut. I knew her in school."

Alex leaned in, listening carefully. Despite everything, he found himself trusting this woman. He took a deep breath, filling his lungs for the questions he wanted to ask her about his mom, but Safa cut him short.

"Your mother had been offered a grant to study Hatshepsut – very prestigious," she said. "But she'd just had you, you see, and she declined."

"She had to give up her grant?" said Alex.

"You were quite sick at the time," said Safa.

"Yeah," said Alex, looking down at his feet. "That sounds like me." *Sick . . . and already causing her trouble.*

Safa smiled sympathetically. "The grant did not go to waste," she said. "I'd planned to do my postdoc work on Ramses VI. Do you know what she told me?"

Alex shook his head, still not looking up.

"She said that the world needs another paper on Ramses like Giza needs another tourist. And then she recommended me to the grant administrator, Dr Alshuff."

"Mahmoud Alshuff?" asked Todtman.

Safa nodded. "Alshuff had been Maggie's doctoral adviser, as well. He trusted her recommendation. And so I found myself studying a woman who took power without apology. A woman whose legacy was too big to be erased by men. Studying Hatshepsut changed what I thought about my country, my history, myself. So, yes, Alex Sennefer, you are welcome to stay here. You and the doctor and" – she looked over at Ren – "your better half."

Then she turned and continued out of the room. "Now, if you'll excuse me, I must go. Bubbi will show you to your rooms once you're done in here. I have a videoconference to get back to."

"But it's the middle of the night," said Alex.

"Not in Tokyo," she said, giving them a small

over-the-shoulder wave and closing the door behind her.

"I like her!" said Ren.

"She is an interesting woman," said Todtman, his voice betraying his admiration.

"How do you know her?" said Ren.

"I have advised her for years on her purchases," said Todtman, pulling up a chair as Alex and Ren collapsed on either side of a sleek modern couch. "Whether the pieces are real, how much to pay, how likely she is to get arrested for having them. . . It is a relationship based on trust."

Alex leaned back into the soft black leather as he listened. A relationship based on trust – and on an opportunity he'd cost his mom. Her first sacrifice for him. He pictured a little web of connections – Todtman, Safa, the university – with his own mom at the centre.

"So what next?" said Ren.

"Tomorrow we go to the university," said Todtman. "And talk to her old adviser."

"Dr Alshuff," said Alex. He was in the web, too.

Todtman nodded. "I know Mahmoud. In fact, I believe I owe him money."

An hour later, they were all sound asleep. It had been an intense day, both physically and mentally.

Around the house, Bubbi and another man watched carefully, peering out windows and into monitors. They knew these guests brought danger with them. But neither man saw the tall regal woman in the front garden, her feet leaving no prints in the soft soil.

She was not seen for the simple reason that she did not want to be, and she left no prints for the simple reason that she was not actually touching the ground.

Instead, she hovered there among the fragrant herbs, staring up at the second floor with half a face.

SCHOOLED

Their hostess was nowhere in sight the next morning, but a traditional Egyptian breakfast was waiting on the kitchen counter downstairs: three plates of fava beans – some whole, some mashed, all cold – with thick pita bread tucked along the sides. "What is this?" asked Ren, grabbing the nearest plate and shovelling some of the beany mix into a pita.

"It is called *fuul*," said Todtman, doing the same.

"Fuel?" said Ren.

"Close enough," said Todtman.

Alex looked around for doughnuts or Pop-Tarts before reluctantly picking up the third plate. He watched the others devour their food without injury and took a bite. Earthy and bitter, the *fuul* tasted like a combination of hummus, lemon and something grittier. He took another bite. Then another. It wasn't so bad, actually. Alex wolfed down his second overstuffed pita and burped. Ren gave him a disapproving look, but Todtman ignored it and said, "Let's go. The university will be open by now."

As soon as they stepped out the door, they saw Safa and Bubbi standing next to the rental car in the driveway, their eyes on a small electronic sensor in Bubbi's hands. Finally, he looked up and shook his head: *No.* Safa walked straight towards them and met them halfway down the walkway.

"No tracking devices," she said. "At least none that we could detect."

"Oh!" said Todtman, an involuntary exclamation that told them all that the possibility hadn't occurred to him.

Safa gave him a sympathetic look. "Sometimes I think you actually live in the ancient world, Doctor."

"Sometimes I wish I did," he said with a slightly abashed smile.

The well-travelled old rental car started on the second try. The gleaming security gate seemed to kick the sputtering clunker out with some disdain, hissing open and then shutting with a loud thunk.

"Who'd want to track this hunk of junk?" said Ren from the back seat.

Alex smiled, but his eyes were alert. They were out in broad daylight in a major Egyptian city. The Order's influence was everywhere in Egypt, and this particular hunk of junk held three very wanted individuals. He felt better in fast-moving traffic. It would be hard to see his face at that speed, and apart from that, he didn't really stand out from the crowd around them. He'd inherited a lot of his father's Egyptian features, even if he'd never known the man.

He looked around the car. Ren's eyes barely topped the rear windows, but Todtman couldn't have stood out more if he was wearing bright green lederhosen.

They'd arrived in Alexandria at night, and now he sized it up by daylight. History revealed itself in layers from block to block. Some stretches were distinctly Egyptian, with mosque minarets needling upward. Other areas were almost European, like a faded, peeling version of the pastel beauty he'd seen in Vienna. And now and then, in between buildings and avenues, he caught sun-sparkling glimpses of the massive blue Mediterranean beyond.

A chorus of car horns erupted all around them as the traffic on the street came to a halt. As Alex looked around for the problem, the horns were drowned out by the sound of an approaching siren. He swung back around in time to see a fire engine roar into view in front of them.

"Where's the fire?" said Ren, ducking her head between the front seats.

The crowd began to scatter on the sidewalk up ahead, and Alex heard shouts in Arabic and a few screams. As the last pedestrians ducked into nearby doors or rushed out into the stopped traffic, he finally saw the cause of the commotion: a ragged mummy, stumbling down the centre of the sidewalk!

Three firefighters appeared behind it, running fast despite their heavy coats. As the first of them approached the ancient corpse from behind, he began pumping feverishly on the sort of small metal canister used to spray chemicals on lawns.

"Are they going to, um, fertilize it?" said Ren, retreating slightly into the back seat.

The creature began weaving unevenly between the sidewalk and the edge of the road. The screams coming from within the cars were more muted now, as any open windows were rapidly raised. The mummy was just a few car-lengths away, and Alex could see its dry wrappings flapping loosely in the morning breeze and one skeletal foot bent nearly backwards. The fireman gave the canister one more pump and then pointed the little nozzle. Clear liquid sprayed forth, dousing the mummy's back.

"BROAN!" it cried hoarsely. "STAHK!"

It turned around and faced its pursuers. The eyes of the man with the spray can turned into wide white-rimmed circles, and he began mumbling prayers, but still he pointed the nozzle. He doused the mummy's front, then tucked the nozzle and ran as the thing stumbled towards him, arms out, bony fingers reaching for living flesh. The second firefighter turned and ran, too. The third prepared to bolt, but before he did, he tossed a small glowing object towards the lumbering corpse.

FOOOF!

The mummy went up in flames. It roared angrily and took a few more steps before collapsing facedown in the street.

The firefighters rushed back, not with gas this time but with a long hose from the truck. They waited until the dried-out corpse was little more than ash before turning the hose on. Ash and steam and scraps of aged linen rose up into the morning sun.

The pedestrians reappeared from the doors and walked almost casually around the remains as the firefighters coiled their hose. The honking resumed. "It appears that they have seen this before," said Todtman as the fire truck pulled away and the traffic began moving again.

Alex had never seen firefighters *start* a fire before – much less by lighting a desiccated corpse – but the world was changing. He remembered the angry, haunted streets of Cairo. The dead there had been only whispers, voices. Now they were part of the morning rush hour.

As the car picked up speed, they lowered the windows again. The warm, slightly salty breeze felt good as they rolled through the city, their eyes peeled for mummies or Order operatives. From her perch in the back seat, Ren saw Alex's head swivelling from side to side, like an electric fan. Scanning the sidewalk, always on the lookout.

She knew he'd been joking about the "little sister" thing, but he really did treat her like one sometimes. He was so determined that he sometimes took on more responsibility than he should. *Don't say you have first watch if you can't stay awake*, she thought, staring at the back of his head. What if that thing had attacked her? She was pretty sure he would've slept through the whole thing. And it definitely wasn't the first time he'd bitten off more than he could chew and got them into trouble. Yeah, he knew a lot about ancient Egypt. Yeah, he was good with his scarab.

But he wasn't the only one who knew things, who could *do* things. She glanced down at her ibis. It had allowed her to zap that shadow, and it had shown her this city. *Was she really getting better with it?*

Ren didn't believe in luck; she believed in probability. When she used the amulet, it still felt like rolling the dice. It had failed her before. Still, it was nice to have a few wins under her belt. For now, she reached up and tucked the ancient artefact under her shirt, careful not to hold it too tightly and invite more images in.

As for Alex. . . She glanced towards the front seat. He had his entire head out the window now, like a wind-drunk dog. She smiled. It was hard to stay mad at him. *But if he messes up again*, she thought, *it will get a lot easier.*

They reached the university, found a parking spot in the visitors' lot, and walked towards the main building, a massive redbrick structure. Even in the middle of the summer, students and professors were walking by, carrying books and having intense conversations. And not just in Arabic. Ren caught snatches of English and French and other languages she didn't know. Not yet, anyway.

As a girl who'd been browsing college websites since fourth grade, she felt, if not at home, then at least more at ease. She remembered her dad's words: *Negativity accomplishes nothing, unless you're an ion.* She wasn't a subatomic particle, and they had work to do. They pushed through the big double doors of the administration building.

"We're going to stop them," she said with a sudden rush of optimism. The mid-morning heat faded inside the cool, hushed hallway.

Todtman, who seemed to know these hallways, looked over at her. "Oh yes?" he said, his expression somewhat bemused.

"Yes," she said firmly, spreading her arms to take

65

in their scholarly surroundings. "Because we're smarter."

Alex agreed immediately. "Those are some ignorant individuals," he said. He looked over at Ren and added, "My mom went here." His eyes were wide with wonder. He pointed emphatically down at the marble-tiled hallway. "She probably walked *right here!*"

Todtman brought the group to a halt in front of a heavy wooden door. A little plaque beside it read ROOM 111-B, DR ALSHUFF. "This is it," he said.

He knocked three times with the rubber tip of his cane.

Puhnk! Puhnk! Puhnk!

"Willkommen!" a voice called through the door.

Clearly, they were expected.

What Ren had no way of knowing as they walked into the sunny, book-lined office was that the old professor within wasn't the only one expecting them.

A FLY ON THE WALL

Dr Alshuff had had it rough.

The old academic stood and greeted them with a forced smile and a black eye. "It is good to see you again, my old friend," Alshuff said to Todtman, but he sounded more nervous than happy.

Alex stared at the ugly purple bruise on the loose skin around the old man's left eye. "And you!" said the doctor, turning and catching him looking. "You look just like—" Alex's ears perked up. He knew he didn't look much like his mom, and he had never seen so much as a picture of his father – but had this man? "Um, just like I imagined," Alshuff added after an awkward pause.

Alshuff extended his hand and Alex shook it. He'd trusted Safa immediately, almost despite himself, but trust was still in short supply in Alex's world. And he didn't trust this nervous, shifty-eyed guy at all. "What happened to your eye?" he said bluntly.

Alshuff immediately launched into an elaborate story involving a heavy book, a top shelf and some dust. Alex couldn't help thinking about his cousin. During the time they'd spent together in London and Egypt, Luke had fooled Alex completely. Alex had fallen for his act, thinking they were allies – even friends – all while Luke was spying on him and Ren. But he wasn't so naive any more. Alex's expression hardened. He was more alert now, more wary – and he was sure Alshuff's story was a lie.

Meanwhile, Alshuff had turned towards Ren. "And who is this?" he said.

"I'm Renata Duran," she said. "Is this school hard to get in to?"

The old professor released a dry, clucking laugh. "Not for an Amulet Keeper," he said, eyeing her ibis. Ren nodded, making a mental note.

Alshuff took a seat behind his big wooden desk and the others pulled out the three chairs arrayed in front of it. "So," he said. "How can I help you today?"

A smile formed above Todtman's sloping chin as he considered the man. Alex could tell he'd picked up their host's phony vibe, too, and he was glad. "As I mentioned on the phone," said Todtman, "we are looking for information about Maggie."

Alshuff shooed a fly away from his face with a wave of one sweaty palm. "Of course," he said. "And what is it you would like to know about her?"

"Ah," said Todtman. "That is the question. We are looking for anything that might help us understand where she is now, where she would go. We believe she's in Egypt, and we know she has history in Alexandria. Beyond that. . ." Todtman let his words trail off, but Alshuff was quick to offer his own.

"You are trying to find her," he offered. "And she does not want to be found."

"Exactly," said Todtman.

Alex looked from one man to the other. There was something going on between them, something extra being communicated in their looks. Alshuff swatted at the fly again, harder this time. Todtman watched him closely.

"Well," said Alshuff, leaning back in his chair, "as you know, Maggie was primarily interested in the Ptolemaic period, when the Greeks ruled Egypt."

He raised his voice as he said this, and Alex got the annoying impression that it was for his benefit. *He knew what the Ptolemaic period was!* It was funny, though: He didn't really remember his mom being particularly interested in it. She rarely even ventured over to the Greek section at the Met.

"You might want to take a closer look at some of the major Ptolemaic sites," Alshuff continued. "The Temple of Philae, perhaps. She would be quite at home in that area, I think."

Alshuff's voice was loud but shaky, dotted with little pauses as if making it up as he went along. His eyes were on the ceiling, his desk – anywhere but on the people he was talking to. Alex had heard enough of his lies. "But my mom never—" he began.

Alshuff cut him off immediately. "Well!" said the old professor, filling his voice with false confidence. "I wish I had more time to talk, but it is a busy day here, and we have a departmental meeting in a few minutes." He pushed his chair back and stood up. "One of our mummies was apparently burned to ashes downtown, and they will want to remind us again to lock our doors."

Todtman pushed back his own chair and stood. Alex and Ren followed suit. Alshuff came around the desk and put his hand on Alex's shoulder. Alex flinched. The gesture seemed friendly enough, but he was also gently but firmly guiding him towards the door. Alex looked up and saw Alshuff looking down at the scarab beneath his collar.

"It has been a very long time since I have seen the Returner," he said, his voice suddenly quite steady. *This*, thought Alex, *is what the man really sounds like*. "Your mother's most significant discovery. Until recently, of course."

Alex looked up at him. "You mean the Lost Spells?"

Alshuff gave him a look he couldn't interpret: Sad? Patient?

A buzzing grew in Alex's right ear, and he reached up and swatted at the fly. Missed it. They were almost to the door now.

"Oh, one more thing," said Alshuff, his voice soft and casual. "You might take a look at her dissertation. I doubt it will offer any more than I have already told you, but you might find it interesting. It should be in the main library, along with her notes. Tell them I sent you."

He took one last look at the scarab as the three guests filed out of the office. "With such an impressive pedigree," he said quietly to Alex, forcing a smile, "I wouldn't be surprised if you found a space already set aside for you in there." Then he turned to Todtman. *"Danke, Doktor."*

And with that, Alshuff swung the door shut.

Todtman stopped it with his good foot. "One more question," he said. "Do you still host the department's poker night?"

Alshuff gave a quick grin, this one somehow more genuine than the others. "Every Friday," he said. Todtman nodded and removed his foot, and Alshuff slammed the door for good.

The friends headed down the hallway towards the nearest exit. The fly, Alex couldn't help but notice, came with them.

"That dude was lying through his teeth," said Alex once they'd put some distance between themselves and Alshuff's office.

"Definitely shady," agreed Ren.

"And what was all that Ptolemaic stuff?" said Alex. "My mom was always going on about the Middle Kingdom, the Early Kingdom – the *Egypt* part of ancient Egypt. I mean, I seriously doubt the Lost Spells were written in Greek!"

Alex looked up to see if Todtman would weigh in on his "old friend," but the German seemed lost in thought. So Alex pushed open the big exit door and squinted into the bright sunlight.

"And he was just so bad at it," continued Ren as they headed across a wide courtyard. "He was practically sweating bullets, wouldn't make eye contact. That guy is a horrible liar."

"But that's the thing," said Todtman, his cane thumping softly beside him as he walked. "He is a terrific liar."

"Uh, are we talking about the same guy?" said Alex.

"Yes," said Todtman. "I have lost many games of poker to that man. He is notorious. You can never tell what he is thinking. His expression never betrays him. He is well known for it in . . . certain circles."

"Wait," said Ren. "Is he a member of your, what do you call it, book club?"

"That is what *you* call it," Todtman pointed out.

"We consider ourselves more of an international association of scholars."

Alex tried to wrap his brain around that. *How could that shifty old dude be a member of the same secret group as Todtman?*

His mom had been a member, too, but now she seemed to be playing a dangerous game all her own. He didn't know what the objective of that game was, but he knew that, just like in poker, deception was key.

"So, should we check out that temple he mentioned, or what?" said Alex, trying to figure out if this whole thing had been a waste of time.

"No," said Todtman. "You are right, he was lying about that. Maggie was never very interested in the Ptolemaic Dynasty – she doesn't even speak Greek."

"Do most Egyptologists speak Greek?" said Ren.

"The ones who are interested in that period do," said Todtman. "As they say in Athens, *Mía glóssa then íne poté arketí.*"

"Uh, sure," said Ren. "So, he was lying and, what? He wanted us to *know* he was lying? Why?"

"I don't think he was speaking entirely for our benefit," said Todtman.

Alex remembered the black eye. "Maybe

The Order has already been here," he said. He remembered Alshuff's raised voice, practically shouting "Temple of Philae". "Maybe they still are. Maybe he thought they were listening in somehow."

Alex swung his head all around as they reached the edge of a large courtyard. *No one behind them.* Todtman led them down a narrow walk between two old redbrick buildings. "This way," he said.

"Where are we going?" said Alex.

"I think perhaps it was the other place he mentioned that we are meant to go," said Todtman.

"The one he mentioned *quietly*," added Ren.

Now Alex got it, too: "The one he said wasn't very important."

Todtman nodded: "Her old dissertation, in the library."

"Gah!" blurted Ren, slapping down hard on her neck. "This fly is driving me crazy!"

That thing is persistent, thought Alex. They turned the corner and he saw a large, six-storey building rising into view. This place had *library* written all over it.

"Let's see what she was really studying – and, more importantly, where," said Todtman, eyeing the impressive structure. "Whatever is in these files represents her roots in this country – a paper trail of her first years here. But keep your eyes open and your amulets ready." And on that note, they entered the cool, hushed world of the central library. The swirl of air as the doors opened caused the persistent little fly to tumble end over end, and the doors closed before it could recover. It landed on the glass and peered in with its many-sectioned eyes. Then, finally, it buzzed off.

SHELF-ISH BEHAVIOUR

"Whoa, this place is huge," said Alex. "There are *miles* of books."

"It's so beautiful," said Ren.

Alex looked over and thought, not unkindly, *Nerd*.

A guard near the entrance looked at them sceptically and asked to see their university IDs.

"Dr Alshuff sent us!" proclaimed Ren, standing on tiptoes so that more than her head was visible above the top of the man's tall desk.

But the guard's interest in their credentials had already vanished – the moment Todtman had wrapped his hand around his amulet. "We are visiting scholars," he said. That seemed true enough to Alex. He and Ren, for example, were in middle school. "And we are expected." That seemed true enough, too: Alex just hoped it wasn't by The Order.

"Of course," said the man, as if talking in his sleep.

They headed towards the information desk.

"I am a professor from Berlin," Todtman said to the young lady behind the desk. He left his amulet out of it this time, but made his normally faint accent almost comically thick. "I need to see the dissertation and notes of one of my colleagues."

The graduate student looked up at Todtman and then down at Alex and Ren. "Yes," she said. "Professor Alshuff told me to expect you. You are looking for an older file, I believe. Those files are in the archives now. Please follow me." She stood up. "My name is Hasnaa, by the way."

Hasnaa led them to the elevator bank and pressed DOWN. She moved with calm confidence, completely at home here. Like so many things, it reminded Alex of his mom. He wondered if she'd also worked in the library when she was studying here.

Everyone else was going up, so they were the only ones who got in when the door dinged open with the down arrow lit up above it. Hasnaa pulled out a key chain and flipped it around until she was holding a very small key. Alex had one just like it for the elevators at the Met. She put the key in its slot at the bottom of the panel, turned it, and then pressed the button that read BASEMENT ARCHIVES: STAFF ONLY.

It lit up in red and they began to descend.

"Uh, are there any other exits?" said Alex, not sure how much of the sinking feeling in his gut was coming from the elevator. "In case of, like" – *an Order ambush* – "a fire?"

Hasnaa gave him a curious look. "There are stairs, of course," she said. The elevator bumped to a stop and the doors slid open. Hasnaa stayed inside as the others got out.

"Here you are," she said. "But please, no fires."

"It's not here," said Ren.

"Are you sure?" said Alex, leaning in to look over her shoulder.

"Now you're in my light," she protested. "But yes, I'm sure."

She'd been given the job of checking not because she was diligent and detail-oriented, although she was both, but because her small stature and nimble fingers were perfect for searching the overstuffed bottom shelf. She flipped through the files one more time to be sure: BATTAR, BATTEN... And then straight to BAVALAQUA.

"No *Bauer*," she confirmed. "But there is something odd..."

"What?" said Alex, leaning in and casting everything into shadow again.

Ren sighed deeply.

"Oh, right," said Alex, stepping back.

Ren eyed the little gap in the files. It seemed strange, considering how jammed the rest of these shelves were. Old, yellowing paper and dry manila folders spilled out like overgrown plants. She touched the gap with her finger. No dust. Then she reached in with both hands and pushed Batten's file away from Bavalaqua's. She peered into the space beyond. It was dark back there, so she raised her amulet, not to ask it questions or offer more inscrutable images but just for...

A flash of brilliant white light lit the space – and told Ren what she needed to know. Boxes of additional material were stacked behind the archaeology department dissertations. Notes, fieldwork, maybe the occasional bone fragment or piece of pottery... She wasn't sure, exactly, but she could see the spot where a large box had been plucked out like a bad tooth.

"The file's gone," she said. "Someone took it."

She stood up and brushed her dusty hands on her shorts. "I guess Alshuff told The Order first," said Ren. "And now they have it."

She looked over at Alex and Todtman. They both looked like they'd just been slapped. "I never thought Alshuff would betray us," muttered Todtman. "Even fearing for his life..."

"Betrayed," mumbled Alex. "But I thought..." He let his voice trail off, and then Ren saw him shake his head hard, like he did sometimes. "There's got to be something else. It really seemed like he was trying to tell us something."

"Yeah," said Ren. "He was telling us to go to the library – but the file is gone."

Alex looked down at the floor, "We must be missing something..."

Ren decided to ignore him this time. It was a dead end, and they needed to let it go. Determination without information just got them into trouble. But his hangdog expression bothered her – and now that she thought about it, Alshuff had said something else. She remembered, because the comment had made her slightly jealous.

"Well," she said, sighing, "he did say that weird thing about you having a spot down here someday."

Todtman stared at her.

"What?" she said.

"Not someday," he said. "*Now.*"

Ren searched her memory banks for the exact words: "He said, *I wouldn't be surprised if you found a space already set aside for you.*"

"Yeah," said Alex. "A spot set aside for me. That's what he wanted us to find. I knew it!"

Ren looked at him, goggle-eyed. "*You* knew it?"

Alex shrugged. "OK, *you* knew it – but I suspected!"

A spot set aside for Alex Sennefer... Ren headed straight for the shelf that held the S's. Unfortunately for her, it was the top shelf this time. *Maybe if I stand on my tiptoes...* Todtman brushed past. "I think perhaps I should handle this one," he said.

"Fine." She sighed. Everyone told her she was due for a growth spurt, and all she had to say to that was *WHEN?* She was getting pretty sick of coming up short.

She squinted up at the faded labels.

"I see a *B!*" whooped Todtman. "Yes, here it is!"

He reached in to pull out several thick folders.

"Hold this," he said, shoving them behind him.

Alex grabby-handed them away from Ren. "Let me see," he said.

Ren leaned in for a look of her own.

"You're in my light!" he chirped.

Meanwhile, Todtman was staring up at the top of the bookcase. The boxes of notes and supporting materials for the files on the upper shelves were piled on top of the case. Ren began to scan the names on the boxes: old black marker on old brown cardboard. "There!" she said, pointing.

And there it was, the name of the woman everyone was looking for, hidden in plain sight behind a simple veil of alphabetical misdirection.

"*Prima!*" exclaimed Todtman. *Awesome.*

A moment later, his hand closed around his falcon amulet, and the chunky old box floated free and drifted feather-like to the floor.

PICTURES FROM THE PAST

They got to work immediately, hauling the box and files over to a little cluster of desks in the middle of the room. The lights hummed overhead and even the tall shelves seemed to lean in for a closer look as Alex carefully peeled back the dry old tape holding the top of the box shut. It came off with only the faintest whisper of protest.

Next to him, Todtman and Ren split the files containing the hefty dissertation and finished papers in half. That seemed like a good place to start for the two more academically minded members of the group. Alex was happy to do the dirty work.

He peered inside the old box and pawed through the top layer with his hands. In jumbled piles and half-spilled files, in ziplock baggies and Tupperware tubs lay his mother's fieldwork. There were notes and photos and bits of carved stone and pottery pulled from the Egyptian ground.

Alex wished he knew what he was looking for. Could she have come here? Snuck a note for him into the box? Or would he have to be on the lookout for something less obvious? He began pulling stuff out and arranging it on top of the nearest desk, trying to make some sense of the jumbled mess.

Unlike the neatly typed pages Todtman and Ren were poring over, the papers Alex found were often handwritten: notes and dates and circles and underlines. "BIG DISCOVERY!" was written in fat, dull pencil at the top of one page. The rest of the page was taken up with numbers – coordinates, maybe, or measurements? Alex wasn't sure, but he set that one aside, anyway.

He picked up the largest of the Tupperware containers and peered through the opaque plastic at the ancient pottery shards inside.

Alex's head swam as he went through the old material. He tried to focus and be rational instead of emotional. More than once he asked himself: *What would Ren do?* She was sitting just a few feet away, of course, but was far too absorbed power-skimming the old dissertation to talk.

He glanced over and saw the title page, set carefully aside on the top corner of Ren's desk: BURIED SECRETS: THE LOST – AND FORBIDDEN – ASPECTS OF MIDDLE KINGDOM FUNERARY RITES. *Now* that *sounded like his mom.*

But his attempts at an even-keeled approach capsized among the messy piles. Going through the materials in the box felt too personal for that. Even in grad school, his mom's distinctive handwriting had already taken shape. The precise, sharp-edged capital *A*'s Alex knew so well shared the page with little loop-de-loop *e*'s and the guesswork mystery of her nearly identical *g*'s and *q*'s.

Sometimes, it was thrilling. *Could this note on hotel stationery be a clue to his mom's current location? Or this unsent postcard from the temples at Abu Simbel?*

And all of it – all of it – felt dangerous. Pushing through these old papers and baggies of little clay statuettes and unlabelled, unexplained stone fragments felt risky, as if somewhere in all of it was a single poisoned pin... Because if they did find something that led them through the decades and straight to her, what then?

He'd had these thoughts before, but they felt closer now, more possible: His mom had always looked out for him, always done what was best – and necessary. If he needed to go to the doctor again, she took him. It didn't matter if he'd just got back or if he begged her to wait. She made the tough calls, and she'd always been right. *So what about now?*

You are trying to find her, Alshuff had said. *And she does not want to be found.* He was telling the truth then, too. It was hard to keep ignoring that fact while they were pawing through her old work. Still, as he zipped a plastic bag closed, he wished he could seal those thoughts up with it.

We need to find her, he told himself for the one-hundredth time. *We need to find the Spells.* The entire world depended on it – *She just doesn't realize how high the stakes are.* That had to be it.

Or maybe she knows exactly... He shook his head hard to dislodge the thought. This one was so sharp that it caused the contents of the folder he'd just picked up to spill out. Old photos went everywhere, some on his desk and some on the floor. The others looked over.

"Ooooh," said Ren. "Pictures."

Clearly tired of reading, she stood up and headed over. *How long had they been at this?* Alex wondered. He'd been so wrapped up in the process that he wasn't exactly sure. He looked down at the scattered snapshots along the desk's edge. And there she was, looking up at him, the woman who would become his mom. She looked so much younger: her cheeks fuller and her skin red from the sun, but it was unmistakably her.

It was like looking at pictures from a family vacation he hadn't been invited to. And then he saw a shot of her leaning over to inspect a hole in the ground. Even wearing a loose, untucked shirt, the bulge in her belly was clearly visible. *He'd been there after all.*

Ren reached over and grabbed the photo, along with a handful of others. "The dates are written on the back," she said. "We should put them back in order. Because *somebody* dropped them."

*

Time slipped by unnoticed down in the sunless, shadow-cornered archive. Once the box was empty, Alex stared down at the piles he'd made on the table. He'd hoped he'd see something that would jog his memory, some secret clue that only he would know. But there'd been no lightning bolts of recognition, no revelations. He'd ended up sorting the carefully labelled pages and pictures and pieces by place. He'd made big stacks for Alexandria, Cairo, Luxor and the Valley of the Kings – places they had already been – and another pile for Abu Simbel to the south. Then there were smaller stacks: Edfu, Minyahur, Aswan.

Was his mom in one of these places? He'd heard her mention many of them – but then, she was an Egyptologist. Cairo came up all the time at work. She'd once brought him a King Tut T-shirt from the Valley of the Kings. Was that a clue, or just a T-shirt?

He looked down at the less-familiar piles. Aswan sounded familiar, and he was pretty sure he'd heard his mom mention Minyahur. He chased the memory but it sped away like an NYC taxi.

Todtman and Ren came over to see his work.

"Find anything?" said Ren.

"I'm not sure," he admitted, unable to keep the disappointment out of his voice.

"Ren," Todtman said. "Perhaps if you used the ibis? With all this information in front of us, it could carry us the last step."

Alex watched Ren's expression carefully, but she had a pretty good poker face herself. He hoped she could help, but he knew her amulet was tricky. It flashed fast-forwarded images into her mind. Sometimes they were clues, and sometimes they were warnings – and sometimes she couldn't tell the difference. Still, what choice did they have now?

"OK," she said.

She took one last look at the piles. Then she took a deep breath, reached up for her amulet and closed her eyes. A moment later, she gasped and opened them.

"What did you see?" Alex said.

She turned to him, blinking to refocus on the world around her. "Nothing," she said.

Alex frowned, annoyed. He knew Ren didn't like to be wrong, but if she wasn't sure, they could help her puzzle out the images. "Come on," he said. "You can tell us."

She looked him in the eyes. "No, really, there was

nothing. I asked it which of these piles was right, and I just got, like, a *blank*."

"Has that ever happened before?" said Todtman.

Ren shook her head. "Never. Sometimes I don't understand what it shows me, but it has always shown me *something*."

Todtman nodded. "Maggie's location could be masked somehow, protected." He sized up the stacks of papers and pictures. "OK," he said. "There will be no shortcuts. We need to go through everything again. We must ask ourselves: Where would she go, when everyone was looking for her? Where would she feel safest? Let's forget about the places we have already been for now and concentrate on what is new."

He leaned forward and pushed the large piles for Cairo, Alexandria, Luxor and the Valley of the Kings farther back.

Alex looked at the remaining piles: Abu Simbel, Edfu, Minyahur, Aswan. He'd heard of the famous tombs at Abu Simbel and knew his mom had mentioned Edfu and Minyahur. A memory flashed by, yellow and grey, but he still couldn't pin it down. And why did Aswan sound so familiar? He reached for that stack, but Ren got it first. He sat down by the Minyahur pile instead, and began going through the pictures.

He picked up a photo of his mom sitting in the sand in front of a campfire with a big metal cup in her hand. It was early evening and a teakettle was set up above the fire. He looked at her face. She was relaxing after a long day. He lingered over it a little too long and Todtman leaned over to see what he'd found.

"It's nothing," said Alex, slightly embarrassed, "just a shot from camp."

Todtman looked more closely. "It's funny, I never saw your mother drink tea."

"Mostly she drank coffee," Alex said. "For the caffeine. She was so busy all the time. But every once in a while, she drank tea. There's this one old brand she likes. I forget the name, but it has a purple flower on the label. Sometimes ... at home ... she..."

He could barely get the words out. He was chasing that elusive memory: yellow and grey...

He was sick that day, and her arms were full...

Of what? When? Why?

He heard Ren rummaging through the papers, but he didn't dare look over. *He was so close...*

"Alex?" said Todtman.

"Sometimes she would drink it to relax at home."
And as soon as Alex said "home," he remembered.
They'd been heading home. He could see it clearly.

"I remember now," he said, and the others leaned
in a little closer.

"Remember what?" said Todtman.

"It was a rainy day." His voice was far away, lost
in the memory. "Mom left work early to take me to
the doctor – again – and she'd brought a big stack
of work home with her. We were waiting to cross
Third Ave., and a taxi went by too close to the kerb."

"Did you get splashed?" said Ren. "I hate that."

"Yeah, exactly," said Alex. "We got blasted with a
big puddle of garbage-water, like the kind where you
can see the oil floating on the surface."

"Nasty," said Ren.

"So nasty," said Alex. "And Mom got the worst
of it. I remember looking over and seeing her just
hugging the soaked files to her raincoat with a look
on her face like *I give up.*"

"It sounds like a very bad day," said Todtman.
"But I'm afraid I'm not following."

"Yeah," agreed Ren. "What's your point?"

"It's what she said next. It was kind of under

her breath but I was listening so carefully that I heard it. She looked down at her stained coat and soaked files and said: 'Time to go to Minyahur.' Then we went home and she had a big mug of hot tea."

"Wait!" said Ren. "I saw something in the pictures."

She began pawing her way backwards through the Minyahur pile, and then: "Here it is." She held up another snapshot of his mom. "Look at the label," she said triumphantly.

Alex looked at the picture. It was the same campsite, even the same teakettle, but his mom was standing now, holding up a small alabaster bowl. It must have been the team's prize discovery that day. But Alex wasn't looking at the bowl. He was staring at a small metal container by his mom's boots. It was a tin of loose tea, with a purple flower on its label.

"Let me see the photo," he said.

They all crowded around as he looked at it closely. He liked it because she was smiling. She was holding the bowl high, raised towards whoever was taking the picture.

"She looks happy," said Ren.

"She looks completely comfortable," said Alex. "Like she did at home sometimes."

Todtman eyed the empty expanse of desert behind the campsite. "It's a good location," he said. "Remote and hidden, but familiar to her."

Alex thought about it. When life in the city had got to her, when just for a moment it had all been too much, the place she wanted to go was a little desert village named Minyahur. It was her place to get away from it all. And was there any better phrase for what she was doing now, pursued by both enemies and friends?

Getting away from it all, thought Alex.

But not any more.

A crazy mix of emotions bubbled and swirled inside Alex: excitement and anxiety and loyalty and loss. But the one that bubbled highest was love. "I think this is where we need to go," he said.

Ren turned to Todtman: "You said we were looking for the place she'd feel safest." She pointed to the photo. "This fits the description to a *tea*."

Todtman ignored the pun. "Yes," he said briskly. "Let's pack this up, and we can leave immediately."

Alex slipped the photo into his back pocket, and they began stuffing the material back into the box.

Ren picked up the stack she'd been going through. "Aswan," she said. "Isn't that where the Temple of Dendur is from?"

"Oh yeah," said Alex. The huge, glass-walled room housing the old stone temple was his favourite place in the whole Metropolitan Museum of Art. "That's why that sounded so familiar." He allowed himself a quick smile. For just a fleeting moment, things seemed to make sense. But his smile faded as quickly as it had appeared.

"What is that *smell*?" said Ren. "I think a rat died down here or something."

She reached up and pinched her nostrils, then looked over at Alex for confirmation. His expression wasn't one of disgust, though. It was one of *fear*.

"That's no rat," he said. "I know that smell."

The same words echoed through the maze of shelves behind them. "That's no rat. I know that smell." The voice was an exact match for Alex's, save for a slight buzzing.

The friends wheeled around and saw a nightmare striding towards them. It wasn't the first fly that had followed them that day.

But it was the largest by a good six feet.

PRETTY FLY FOR A BAD GUY

"I knew you were in this building somewhere." The fly spoke in his own voice this time. It was not an improvement. Scratchy and uneven, it made Alex's skin crawl. Actually, everything about the fly bugged him: the way his filthy robes clung heavily to his frame, as if greased; the way the small, strange mouth of his mask puckered and smacked, as if alive.

"Yeah, 'cause that old man told you!" called Ren, doing her best to disguise the fear in her voice.

She quickly turned to Todtman and mouthed: *Not you*. But his attention was divided between the approaching enemy and the piled evidence.

The fly tilted his mask and considered Ren with its bulbous composite eyes. "The old man told me nothing but lies," said the fly, his jagged voice betraying a certain amusement. "A little birdy told me you were here."

He raised his right hand and extended his long, gnarled index finger. But it wasn't a little birdy that landed there; it was a buzzing black dot. The fly perched briefly on the hairy digit before buzzing off.

"That fly. . ." Ren began.

"Was a spy," finished Alex, his eyes beginning to water from the stink.

"You should never trust old men," added the fly, directing the comment towards Todtman.

The elder Amulet Keeper finally tore his attention from the piled papers and focused fully on the fly. Alex's stomach lurched as he realized the reason for Todtman's divided attention: If the fly went through those piles, he'd see they were sorted by place. They were all searching for the same person, and unlike the friends, The Order had the manpower to search all of those places at once. Alex glared at the masked operative. Not only was The Order standing in the way of where they needed to go, they were also a threat to get there first!

"It is not like you to dispense life lessons, Aff Neb," said Todtman, giving this horror a name. "Death is more your style."

Aff Neb's many eyes shimmered like water as they shifted focus. "True," he rasped. "Death tastes better... Let me show you."

Aff Neb's mouth puckered and smacked one more time – and then released a thick stream of greenish-brown vapor. The putrid plume billowed forth, filling the little clearing among the shelves.

"Don't breathe it in!" shouted Alex before slapping his hand over his mouth and nose.

"No kidding!" called Ren, her own eyes bugging out from the approaching grossness.

Just a few feet away now, it smelled more like a thousand sweaty feet. Alex held his breath and shifted his grip, dropping one hand to his amulet and pushing the other out in front of him.

The mystic wind rose up with merciful swiftness, ruffling books and papers all around – and pushing the stink cloud back where it came from.

"Guhh!" Alex gasped. He released the sour

breath he'd been holding and gulped a fresh lungful that smelled like approaching rain.

Aff Neb seemed entirely at home in his own stink. "I see you have been hard at work down here," he said, eyeing the half-full box and remaining stacks of paper. "Tell me, what have you found?"

Alex tried to step between the thousand-eyed gaze and the table, but there were better ways to obstruct the view.

"Hey, fly guy!" called Ren.

Aff Neb's eyes shimmered as they shifted towards her. They had thousands of lenses – but no lids. Ren squeezed her ibis tightly.

FOOOP! A bright-white flash lit the dim basement.

"Grehh!" called the fly, his hands reaching up too late to cover his creepy peepers.

Alex caught some of the flash, too, but before the swirling spots even faded from his vision he was already at the table, dumping the remaining stacks into the old box with both hands. "Got it!" he said, slapping the top closed.

"Let's go!" called Todtman, and the three Amulet Keepers turned to run.

But as they did, Alex caught a glimpse of

movement in the gaps in the bookshelves. In the narrow space between the tops of the old books and files and the shelves above them he saw cloth, arms, legs, a quick flash of metal – *guns!* "Uh, guys," he said as they rushed away from Aff Neb and into the nearest row of shelves.

"I see them," said Todtman.

"What are we going to do?" said Alex. Aff Neb had recovered and was in hot pursuit, and an ambush of Order gunmen awaited them among the rows.

"Get in the clear," said Todtman.

His words came out in a sad, almost wistful sigh, and suddenly Alex knew what he was planning. "Oh no," said Ren, figuring it out, too – and sharing Todtman's academic reservations.

The old scholar wasn't happy about it, but he didn't hesitate. He squeezed down hard on the falcon and grunted slightly with the effort. By the time they reached the narrow gap at the end of the first row, the heavy metal bookcases had already begun falling like dominoes.

Thousands of pounds of bound books and thick files tipped and toppled, and twice as much weight in metal shelves and stacked boxes came down, too.

"GAAARARB!" shrieked Aff Neb as the heavy case they'd just rushed past fell over on him, pinning him against the next case as it fell, too. On either side, Order thugs were squashed like Order bugs. Somewhere in the stacks, a pistol went off, the bang muffled as the bullet buried itself in some old book or other.

Standing in their tiny clearing amid a veritable paper apocalypse, Todtman and Ren cast horrified looks all around. Even Alex was stunned by how fast decades of neatly filed scholarship had been reduced to toppled chaos.

"That is going to take *for ever* to re-alphabetize," moaned Ren.

But even as they surveyed the wreckage, their pursuers began to push free. An arm punched through a stack of books to the left, the sound of shifting, tearing paper was heard to the right, and then: *FOOM!* A stack of books was blown clear up to the ceiling by the telekinetic might of the fly mask.

"There!" said Todtman, pointing to a door along the wall. "The staircase."

Alex and Ren began picking their way over the fallen books and files and shelves. Ren made decent time hopping from one flat spot among the books and boxes to the next, but Alex was carrying a crumpled box of his own and couldn't quite manage the jumps. He hunted for level surfaces to place his feet.

"Hurry, hurry!" called Ren. "I see a gun!"

Alex turned to look. Sure enough, a hand pushed a black pistol through the piled paperwork. Alex used the scarab to send the weapon flipping end over end across the room, but he knew there would be more. They needed to get to the stairs fast, and if this shifting terrain was tough for him, how would Todtman ever manage on one good leg?

"Watch out!" Todtman called as he zoomed past.

Alex stumbled out of the way, then did a double take. Todtman had his hand on his amulet and a book under each foot. Alex couldn't believe it: He was using his amulet to ride the old books like skates, the flat surface of each one hovering a few inches above the scattered debris. He zipped towards the door like a bug skimming across the surface of a pond.

Alex spotted some big books in front of him and looked down at his own amulet. *No way*, he thought. Todtman had had decades to practise with his amulet. If Alex tried, it would be 3, 2, 1: face-plant! Instead, he and Ren hopped and stumbled and hustled across the last half shelf.

Todtman reached the heavy fire door to the stairwell first, and as soon as the other two arrived, he flung it open.

Alex's breath caught in his throat as he stared into the stairwell – and at the wall of guns directly inside.

A row of three tightly packed men stood in the doorway, and there were three more a few steps up, all pointing semiautomatic pistols directly at them. With two barrels pointed at his face, Alex knew that any move towards his amulet would mean death. Or maybe they would just shoot them all, anyway.

"What?" came a jagged voice behind them. "You didn't think we would cover the exits?"

Alex and the others slowly turned to face Aff Neb, the guns that had been pointed at their faces now jabbing into their exposed backs.

"I will take that box now," the fly said. His greasy robes were torn, and it seemed as if all eight thousand lenses in his eyes were brimming with annoyance. Other gunmen were rising from the scattered debris and filling in alongside their leader. Their bodies were battered, their guns were pointed, and they all seemed pretty eager to pull the trigger.

Alex knew better than to anger them now, and yet. . .

He glanced down at the box. It was because of him that the Death Walkers had been released, because of him that The Order's plans had been set in motion. Now he was being asked to hand over the keys to victory, as well.

"Here you go," he said, pulling the heavy cardboard cube out from under his arm and extending it forward.

"Alex!" hissed Ren.

"You mustn't," said Todtman.

He wouldn't. No matter the cost.

As Aff Neb took a step forward, Alex continued the motion, using all his strength to toss the box up towards the ceiling.

"Catch it!" cried Aff Neb.

But as all eyes followed the modest flight of the box, Alex quickly grasped his amulet, thrust out his free hand, and absolutely obliterated the thing with a concentrated spear of whipping wind. The old cardboard was torn to shreds, and the last thing Alex saw was a shower of paper and pictures and pottery scattering through the air and drifting down towards the waiting chaos all around. Towards a floor full of books and paper and pictures and pottery from all the *other* fallen files and boxes.

That ought to keep 'em busy, he thought.

Then the butt of a pistol smashed down on the back of his head and his whole world went dark.

INTO THE PIT

Alex woke slowly. There was a dull pain on the back of his head and the feel of stone beneath him and something gritty on his face and neck. He reached around to touch the sore spot. As soon as his finger pressed into the tender, swollen bump, he remembered how he'd got it.

His eyes opened wide, only to be flooded by harsh light. He forced himself to sit up, and scanned the space above him for Aff Neb or his gunmen. But all he saw were the gently curved walls of a deep round pit and, far above that, a clear blue desert sky.

Where was he? Why —

"Good morning, Alex," he heard. "Or should I say, good afternoon."

Todtman. As Alex turned towards his voice, he was surprised to feel the scarab shift against his chest. *Aff Neb hadn't taken it?*

Todtman was sitting up against the sheer wall of the pit, looking a little worse for wear, his familiar suit jacket and cane nowhere in sight. Ren was seated next to him. Alex felt his tensed muscles relax ever so slightly. He let out a long breath and pulled another back in. "I'm glad you're both OK," he said.

"Are we?" said Ren. "I doubt it. I'm glad you're awake or conscious, or whatever – but it's not like we can go anywhere." She gestured up at the pit.

Alex took a quick look around. The pit had to be forty feet deep and at least as far across, the walls ranging from light tan to bone white. *Limestone*, he thought. *Just like in the Valley of the Kings.* The air was warm, and he reached up and brushed a sprinkling of sweat-stuck sand from his face and neck.

"We're in the desert," he said.

"Yes," said Todtman, wincing as he rose to his feet. "Somewhere in the central desert, if I had to guess. It wasn't an especially long flight."

Flight? thought Alex. He must have been *really* out of it.

"Did they … hurt you?" he asked. It was a dumb question. He could already see a cut above Todtman's left eye and a swollen bump under his right. He'd been roughed up. He quickly glanced over at Ren, relieved to see no visible injuries.

"I may have resisted a little," admitted Todtman, taking a few short steps. Without his walking stick, he limped noticeably on the leg that had been crippled by a scorpion sting during their pursuit of the first Death Walker. He began to slowly move across the pit. Ren popped up beside him. Her ibis and Todtman's falcon were in plain view at their necks. Alex groaned as he climbed to his feet to join them.

"Why didn't they just finish us off back in Alexandria?" he said. They were approaching a new stretch of the pit's gently curved wall, following Todtman's slow progress. Alex had no idea where they were headed. There was no visible means of entrance or exit, no doorway or ladder or rope.

"Yes, that does seem odd," admitted Todtman, coming to a stop. "They may be curious about what we know."

An ice-cold wave washed through Alex. *Minyahur.* "We can't say anything!" he said urgently.

"We may not have a choice," said Todtman, and the ice-cold wave doubled back. Torture. Magic. What lengths would The Order go to? He resolved then and there that they could do what they wanted to him. As much suffering as he had caused, the least he could do was endure some. Besides, he had a lifetime of practice with pain. But it wasn't himself he was worried about. He looked over at Ren.

"But it may not come to that," continued Todtman. He lifted his sloping froglike chin towards a scattering of symbols cut into the wall. The shallow marks were nearly invisible in the light stone.

"Why aren't those cut deeper?" said Alex.

"They were," said Todtman. "But they've worn down through the ages. These symbols are very old – even by Egyptian standards."

"Old Kingdom?" said Alex.

"Indeed," said Todtman. "Close to five thousand years old, if I had to guess."

Instinctively, Alex and Ren closed their hands

around their amulets. Only a moment later, they released them.

"That's weird," said Ren. "Normally, the ibis lets me read hieroglyphs."

Todtman nodded. "As I said, they are very old. Precursors to the hieroglyphs we know today. But I think I can puzzle out a few. Here" – he pointed to the stacked symbols before them and then to another cluster a few yards away – "and there."

"What do they say?" said Ren.

Todtman ran a finger along the shallow groove of the nearest symbol, pursing his lips and taking one last look before delivering his verdict.

"It seems fairly clear to me," he said, "that they brought us here to be..." He pointed at the last symbol in the bottom row. "Do you see that one? Very similar to a common hieroglyph found in nearly every Middle Kingdom tomb."

"Death?" guessed Alex. "Burial?"

"Close," said Todtman. "A sacrifice, an offering."

Alex stared grimly at the symbol, his head reeling with the realization. He felt, for a moment, like he might black out again. It might have spared him some suffering if he had, because he now understood why they'd been left with their amulets. In ancient

Egypt, all sort of things were sacrificed to appease the spirits and please the gods: Everything from animals as large as oxen to treasures of incalculable value.

He looked down at his scarab. The amulets were the priceless treasure.

Then he looked up at his friends, the small, huddled group of three.

And they were the animals.

THEIR VILE HOST

"We must get out of here," said Todtman, peering up at the sky above. "And if we can, they have already taken us almost halfway to our destination."

Alex looked around, trying to calm his racing pulse. They were in deep trouble – literally – but Todtman's presence gave him some extra confidence. They needed to concentrate on escape. But they needed to be smart about it. He remembered the spying fly at the university, and knew that this pit could be bugged in other ways, as well. "So *that place* is close?" he said.

Todtman nodded. "It is in the southern desert."

"Yeah, *if* we can get out," said Ren. "And if we can't, we're toast. Sacrificial toast."

Alex scanned the walls. "There must be a way out somewhere."

"There is an opening," said Todtman. "Three metres up, behind us."

"Yeah," confirmed Ren. "They dropped us out of, like, a door. We had to *catch* you. But I can't find it now."

Alex eyed the stone nine feet up. "I don't see one, either," he said.

"You are not meant to," said Todtman. Where he stood, the shadow from the pit's edge fell across him so that his chest and head were sunlit and everything below that bathed in grey. As Alex watched, the line of shade shifted and grew. There was something moving along the pit's edge!

Alex spun around.

"Mmuh-rack?" The strangely familiar sound echoed clearly through the pit below.

Alex exhaled. It was Ren's undead BFF, the mysterious mummy cat she'd freed from a shattered

114

museum case in London. They'd last seen her in the Valley of the Kings, which, Alex suddenly realized, probably wasn't too far from here.

"Pai!" called Ren, and immediately regretted it. Even forty feet below, they could see the mummy cat gather her haunches underneath herself and prepare to jump. "Don't! Pai! No!" called Ren, but it was too late. The formerly frisky feline had already taken the leap. She whistled down the open air of the pit, legs slightly spread, ancient wrappings rustling.

Ren started forward, like an outfielder approaching a fly ball, but she didn't get there in time. She winced as Pai hit the ground in front of her.

FFLONNK!

Pai flattened out, spread-eagle, on impact. But by the time Ren reached her, the ex-cat was standing in the middle of the small cloud of sand and dust she'd kicked up, licking one bony front paw. "Mmm-rack!" she said as Ren scooped her up.

Alex leaned over to Todtman. "I guess cats really do land on their feet – even undead ones."

Five feet away, Ren took one of Pai's raggedly wrapped front legs in her hand and waved it back at them. "Pai says hi," she said, her fear making her goofy.

The mummy cat immediately leapt from her arms. Pai-en-Inmar, sacred servant of the cat-headed goddess Bastet, had her pride.

Todtman watched the little exchange grimly. "Tell me," he said. "Have you seen this cat out in the daylight before?"

Alex thought about it. "Not usually," he said. "We saw her at, like, sunset once, though. With King Tut."

Todtman's eyebrows lifted at the mention of the boy king. Alex saw it and added: "He was a pretty cool guy. Tough, too – wish he was here to help us now."

"I don't like it," said Todtman.

"Don't like what?" said Ren, who had followed Pai back into their general vicinity.

"Any of it," said Todtman. "A simple mummy was one thing, and the ghostly voices in Cairo had no form. But Pai is a powerful and sacred creature. She used to visit this world only in the dead of night; now she walks in broad daylight. The two of you travelled into the afterlife, and something followed you *out*. Each Death Walker we encounter is more powerful than the last. And Tutankhamun, a pharaoh, a living god, was among us. . ."

"OK, but what does that—" Ren began.

"The Final Kingdom," said Todtman in a hushed tone.

Alex, who had been scanning the pit wall for the hidden door or any other sign of weakness, choked on his own breath. He'd heard the same words on the sun-parched lips of the last Death Walker.

"Wait, what?" said Ren. "Seriously, what?"

Alex explained. He knew his friend hated not being in the know. "It's, like, when the world of the living and the world of the dead join, when the barriers between them open, and. . ." He turned to Todtman. It had been years since his mom had told him the story. "What's the rest?"

Todtman looked down at the mummy cat, sunlight lighting her back. "And life and death wash together like the waters of the Nile."

"So, wait, that's what this is all about?" said Ren, a quick study. "The Spells and The Order and the Death Walkers – and Pai?"

"Mmm-rackk?"

"I think so," said Todtman. The old German's tone remained distant and flat as he spoke, a retreat from his own fear into rationality. "The Spells opened a doorway between the world of the living and the world of the dead. It was a breach, a jailbreak. The Death Walkers were waiting, and they escaped. But now the walls are crumbling, too. The borders are opening. If they do, the worlds will merge and the living and the dead will exist side by side. One kingdom, and one in which The Order and their Walker allies would be unstoppable."

Alex stared down at the hard, sand-dusted floor. His growing guilt dug in with sharp fingers. He kept his eyes down in case the others were looking at him. *That breach had been caused for him, to let him back through...* He felt the sudden overwhelming urge to do something – anything! – to try to repair the damage. *If we could just get to Minyahur,* he thought. "OK, I am not going to die in this pit," he said, desperate for forward motion. "Maybe we can open the hidden door with our amulets... Maybe if I stood on your shoulders..."

Todtman nodded. "Possibly. It is what is behind the door that worries me, but..."

But above them, the doorway was already opening.

The friends turned towards the grating sound

of stone sliding along stone. The doorway swung inward, finally revealing its carefully hidden edges. Disliking the sound, Pai crept away into the shadow cast by the near wall. Alex, on the other hand, eyed the dark opening hungrily. A moment later it was filled by a looming figure.

The man stepped forward, so tall and broad-shouldered that his thick black robes seemed to fill the entire frame. He regarded them through the eyes of a golden mask.

"Another operative," whispered Alex, his eyes transfixed by the pockmarked realism of the mask's golden skin and the iron beak that curved down into a brutal point.

"No," whispered Todtman. "That is their leader."

Alex finally placed the image on the mask. It was an Egyptian vulture, a species that was both fearsome predator and opportunistic scavenger. This man was the leader of the ancient death cult that had hounded them across three continents. And now, he spoke.

"You have come a long way," he said. "You have troubled me more than you know. Weighed on my thoughts."

The vulture mask had two small eyeholes, and

Alex caught a subtle glimmer in the darkness behind them, a flash of white and reflected light. The man's words could apply to any of them, but his eyes were fixed on Alex.

"I should have killed you already, but even now, I am tempted to offer you a deal. Tell me what you know in exchange for your little lives. . ." Alex still felt as if this man was talking directly to him, but a beat later his gaze shifted to take in the others. Looking for takers, he found none – and then he withdrew the offer. "But you would lie to me. I would torture you and stare into your souls – but still you would lie. You Keepers, you act like such heroes, and yet you lie so well. . . It makes me wonder how different we really are."

But he didn't wonder for long. He turned back towards Alex and continued: "I am sorry. But it is over. Soon, we will piece together what you found in that library." Alex glared angrily up at the man. "Your part is done, your struggle is over, but die knowing two things. First, you serve a noble purpose. Your sacrifice will win us the favour, and more control, of a powerful ally. And second, death, as I am sure you understand by now, is only the start of your journey."

Alex caught a glimpse of heavy leather boots,

just visible beneath the hem of the leader's robes. His feet were mere inches from the edge of the doorway. Alex's amulet had thrown a man across a room before. How hard would one good tug be? But as he began slowly sliding his hand up towards the scarab, his fingers began to twitch and spasm. He had lost control of his own hand, and a moment later it jerked back down to his side in one convulsive movement.

"Ah, Alex – Alex Sennefer – I do appreciate the fight. I do. But I assure you, I am in control here." The leader's gaze shifted between Alex and Todtman. Alex's eyes followed, and he saw that Todtman's hands were also twitching slightly at his sides.

The German tried reason instead. "It is a dangerous game you play," he said. "In your rush for power, you are unleashing forces that you can't possibly—"

"Oh, but it is not a game at all," said the leader. "It is deadly serious. And you should know better than to underestimate me." He paused, though Alex couldn't say if it was to savour the moment or mourn it. Either way, the leader ended with a flourish: "Enjoy the other side."

He took one last look at Alex and spun around. The hems of his robes whirled. Alex and Todtman reached for their amulets, but it was too late. Two quick steps had carried the leader back into darkness, and he was gone. Stone ground against stone as the door began to slide closed.

"Stop it!" called Todtman. "Keep it open!"

Alex grasped his scarab hard with his left hand and pushed his right palm straight out at the closing door, directing all the amulet's force against it. Todtman did the same. The door slowed briefly and then...

KHHRUUNNK!

It slammed shut.

"No," gasped Ren as the noise echoed through the pit.

"He is not staying to watch, to take credit," said Todtman, his tone shaken and uneasy. "Whatever is coming scares even him." He turned towards Ren. "You must use the ibis. We must know what we are facing."

Alex was ready to jump in if she needed more convincing, but Ren just nodded. Alex watched her carefully as she took hold of the pale white bird. She'd drawn a blank last time – literally. Would this time be any different? Her eyes closed briefly, and when they opened again, Alex could see the fear in them.

"What is it?" said Todtman.

Alex had a pretty good idea what she was going to say, but he held his breath, hoping he was wrong.

"Death Walker," she breathed.

"Oh no," said Alex. They all understood the danger. The Walkers were powerful ancient entities. Knowing they would fail the weighing of the heart ceremony to gain entrance into the afterlife, they had clung to its edges by sheer force of will, waiting for their opportunity to escape. The only way to defeat one was by using the scarab's power and the right spell from the Book of the Dead – the spell that connected with what the Walker had been in life. But none of that mattered now. They didn't have a copy of the Book of the Dead, not even a single spell, much less all two hundred.

"Did you see anything we can use against it?" whispered Todtman. "Any way to escape?"

Ren shook her head. "It's too late," she whispered. "It's coming." She pointed at the limestone wall to her left, taking a trembling step back as she did.

Alex peered at the pale stone. There was nothing

there, and for once, he hoped his best friend was wrong.

She wasn't.

The wall itself – the ancient, weathered stone – began to shift, to push outward.

A shape began to emerge.

STONE MEETING BONE

Ren watched in horror as the flat stone of the wall began to bulge outward into a bubble of pale stone about six feet up. She didn't realize it was a face until the sunken eyeholes took shape and the neck began to push outward underneath it. Then came the shoulders, then the chest.

The head pulled free of the wall with a wet tearing noise that sounded more like meat than stone. The rest of the body dragged itself free of the wall, leaving no indentation, no indication whatsoever that a section of stone the size and shape of a ragged human body had been removed.

Its steps were stiff and uneven. Chunks of stone flaked off and fell to the ground with each bend and flex. The creature stopped, crossed its stony arms in front of it, and pointed its featureless visage towards the sky above.

There was a soft cracking sound.

"Turn away!" called Todtman, covering his face with his hands and turning his back on the macabre spectacle. As he turned, his bad leg gave out and he crumpled to the ground.

Ren rushed over to help, but as she did, there was a muffled crash – like thunder heard from under a blanket – and rock exploded outward from the Walker. Limestone dust turned the entire pit white, and here and there Ren felt the sting of larger chunks against her skin.

She heard Alex cry out but could see nothing. Her eyes stung from the powdered stone, and when she tried to call Alex's name, thick white dust filled her mouth. She convulsed into hacking coughs and covered her face.

As the heavy dust settled to the ground, she risked a peek back. The Walker's true form was revealed.

It looked like death itself: a ragged mummy – or most of it, anyway. The wrapping was mostly torn away, and some pieces of the body were missing. A few of the fingers were just gone, but the larger gaps had been filled in with clay and pale stone. Half its skull was clay, much of its torso was stone, and none of it quite fit or matched. For eyes, it had two white stones.

And yet it moved. And yet, somehow, it lived. It took a step forward and drew in a long, rasping breath. In the warm desert air of the pit, Ren went cold to the tips of her toes. As the Walker's chest expanded, a few remaining sections of rib rose beneath the shabby wrapping. Even the limestone that made up the rest of its chest seemed to flex and breathe.

Ren, on the other hand, felt as if a horse was sitting on her chest. Fear constricted her breathing. The other Walkers had looked scary, sure, but they'd also looked alive. They'd come back, and they had the skin and clothing to prove it – even if that skin was sometimes burned or swollen.

Todtman spoke softly, his voice coloured by both awe and fear: "This Death Walker is older than the others, beyond ancient. Made when

127

the mummification process was still crude. And whatever he was buried in must have given out. This one's been in the ground. Its body has calcified."

Ren eyed the vein of living limestone in its chest – stone meeting bone – and felt the same sense of unreality she always did when confronted with the brazen illogic of magic. It felt like floating free from the world she knew, with nothing to grab on to, nothing to stop her from floating away so far that she'd never find her way back.

And as the creature took another step forward and Ren took another step back, she realized that it might be true this time. She might never get back to the world she knew: *home*.

Here, at the end, the homesickness that had grown inside her since she left New York became a razor-sharp ache. She'd never sit in the Met again, staring at her beloved Rembrandts and knowing her dad was somewhere nearby. Knowing that she could go ask him for ice cream money or just hang out and watch him work. She realized she'd never have another "girls' day" with her mom, going to Serendipity and getting "drippity" sundaes.

"Marr fesst dol!" croaked the Walker, snapping Ren back to the overheated reality of the pit. Like the others, Ren already had her hand around her amulet. Normally, that allowed them to understand the ancient Egyptian of their adversaries. Not now.

"Can you understand it?" she asked.

"A lost tongue," said Todtman.

Ren peered into the creature's open mouth as it spat out more inscrutable syllables and saw that its real tongue was lost, too, replaced by a thick slab of clay. The thing flicked and curled with the liveliness of a fat brown toad. Ren wanted to vomit.

The Walker took another step forward; the friends took another step back – only to find their backs were nearly to the wall. Soon they would find out what terrible, deadly power this Walker possessed. Unless... Her mind flashed back to midnight in Vienna. If that shadow creature had been out of place in this world, well, then this earthenware weirdo definitely was.

"Stand back!" she said to her friends. "Cover your eyes!"

She squeezed the ibis tight in her left hand and called on its power once more. She thrust out her right hand. There was a quick white flash and then ... nothing. What had seemed so mighty at night amounted to little more than a camera flash in the daylight flooding the pit. The Walker flinched slightly.

And then it attacked.

The Walker rushed forward, its stone-patched legs moving with surprising fluidity. "Split up!" called Ren.

Alex turned to run – and couldn't! He stared down, incredulous. The floor of the pit was solid stone, but he felt his feet sinking down into it as if it were mud. He watched in terror as the stone reached the laces of his boots. He could hear the creature's footsteps heading towards him, and he tried desperately to lift first one leg and then the other. Nothing. He could only squirm as his feet sank farther.

He saw Ren struggling, too. Her head and shoulders turned to rush along the wall, but her lower half refused to follow.

Only Todtman had managed to stay a step ahead. A vine of stone rose up and grabbed the heel of one of his black dress shoes, but with one hand on his amulet, he swept the other downward, shattering the stone shackle.

Alex followed his example, squeezing the scarab

130

hard and then forming his other hand into a fist and smashing it down directly over each foot in a quick one-two. He felt like he'd just dropped a bowling ball on each foot, but he heard two muffled cracks and quickly pulled his feet up through the powdered stone.

He turned and saw that the Walker was just a few yards from Ren now, already stretching out one bony three-fingered hand. Stuck in the floor, all she could do was stare at the approaching horror with eyes gone round with fear.

"No," Alex breathed. He felt a sudden, achingly sharp sense of responsibility for his friend's safety. She had followed him halfway around the world, through one peril after another, and he could not let anything happen to her now. He rushed towards both of them.

"Hey, stone-face," he shouted desperately at the creature. It turned and regarded this new threat with pale eyes. Alex battled back his fear and squeezed his amulet hard, but before he could use it, a slab of stone shot out from the back wall of the pit, like a dresser drawer opening outward. It cracked Alex hard in the side and slammed him to the ground.

He landed with a loud "Ooouff!"

He rolled over and scrambled to his feet. The stone grabbed at him the whole time, but by moving fast, he was able to stay out of its rough grip –

The Walker's shadow fell over him.

Alex stumbled back and to the side to create some space. Left hand on his amulet, Alex pointed the fingers of his right hand into a spear and lashed out at the Walker with a whipping, whistling column of super-charged wind. *If this creature is really of the earth*, thought Alex, *let's see how it handles some erosion!*

Bits of clay and chunks of stone chipped and slipped off. Another finger sheared off the Walker's right hand and went flying end over end out of sight. The ancient menace roared into the unrelenting gale and stumbled backwards a few steps. Alex narrowed his eyes, tightened his fingers and stretched his arm out farther. His head pounding, his body aching from the force channeled through it, he willed the wind to increase.

He stared directly into the two white stones pressed into the clay-patched front of the Walker's skull and saw the evil there. What he did not see, until it was too late, was the creature raising a now two-fingered hand, palm down, and slamming it hard towards the ground.

The pit floor pulsed like the skin of a bongo drum. The force was so strong Alex could feel it in his teeth, and he found himself tossed two feet into the air. He crashed down on his back and smacked the tender bump on the back of his head. Looking up, he saw stars spiralling in the blue sky above.

A moment later, his head cleared.

It was a moment too long. He desperately tried to sit up, to take hold of his amulet again – but he was pulling against stone. The pit floor had already encircled him with its tendrils, and now he felt himself sinking back into it. Legs, arms, pinned.

He was helpless.

Todtman, however, was still free and using his amulet to fight back. A lance of invisible force carved into the creature, blowing a clean, round hole in its torso. Alex's hopes rose, even as his body sank. He heard Ren let out a triumphant "Yes!"

But the Walker didn't so much as look down, and as its next step touched the pit floor, Alex saw limestone flowing like liquid up the creature – from foot to leg to body – filling in the hole. "Oh no," whispered Alex, his arms and legs now fully encased in stone and only his chest, neck and head still above it.

Todtman steeled himself for another attack, his eyes wide, seeking out the next threat. Would it come from below? Behind?

Above.

A chunk of stone no bigger than a baseball broke off the top edge of the pit. There was a faint whistling sound, Todtman looked up, and. . .

KLONK!

The stone hit him smack in the forehead, and he hit the ground like a sack of potatoes. The pit floor immediately encircled and immobilized him.

Alex's heart sank. He had failed both his friends, and he knew what came next. Death Walkers fed on the souls of the living – and they were messy eaters. The earthen entity surveyed its three trapped foes. It watched them struggle uselessly against the pit's stony grip, like a finicky diner perusing a menu, deciding what to eat first.

A flash of white light made up its mind. "No, Ren!" called Alex, but it was too late. The Walker headed directly for her, closing the distance in long, hungry strides. She released another blast of white light. It was weaker this time, and had even less effect. But then —

"Mmmm-rack?"

Pai stepped into view, brushing past Ren's sunken legs and sitting down directly between Ren and the Walker. Alex had forgotten all about Pai. It was easy to do with an enchanted feline who had a habit of vanishing abruptly. But at the moment, Pai wasn't going anywhere.

"Mmm-RACK!" she repeated, not as a question this time.

The mummy cat's vocabulary might not stretch much past one word, but her meaning seemed clear enough: *Over my long-dead body.*

The Walker looked down and opened its mouth. It took Alex a few moments to recognize the hoarse rasp that came out as a laugh.

"No, Pai," Ren said softly. "Go."

Alex saw the tears in his best friend's eyes and felt guilt stab into him again. Others had died on this quest, but he didn't think he could take it if she did. She was only here to help him, and now... He struggled as hard as he could against the stone all around him, jerking one way and then the other. The stone didn't even hint at budging.

"Get out of there, Ren!" called Todtman from his own confinement. "Try to free one foot at a time!"

But the stone was up past Ren's ankles now and

neither foot would budge. Her last line of defence was an undead temple cat – which the Walker now casually flicked aside. He waved his hand and a two-foot-tall wave rose in the stone floor, heading straight for Pai, moving fast.

The mummy cat hissed and raised one bony paw, but the stony wave overwhelmed her. Her small body was carried off and – *SSPLACKK!* – smashed hard into the back wall of the pit. As the stone sank back into the ground, Pai wobbled upright, but she barely had time to look up before the next strike. A ten-foot-tall stone column crashed down on her with enough power to crush a car. As it receded, her little body lay motionless along the wall, bent in ways it should not have been.

"Noooo!" cried Ren.

And then everything changed.

In the middle of a cloudless day, a strange darkness fell over the pit.

VIOLENCE ITSELF

The darkness lifted a moment later, revealing a woman with the head of a cat. She stood in the centre of the pit, considering her surroundings. Everything was quiet and still. The Walker stood perplexed, its crude mouth hanging open. Even the light wind that had played on the warm air of the pit had stopped. The world itself seemed to be holding its breath.

"Shhhhh!" hissed Todtman, before adding in a rushed and barely audible whisper: "Do not move, do not provoke her."

Not moving, Alex could manage. Still lying on his back, sunk up to his neck in stone, he really didn't have a choice. But he could not take his eyes off this . . . this *what*? She had the body of a woman, clothed in a long, sleek gown, but her head was that of a giant cat – the shape of a Siamese but the size of a lioness. The soft fur rippled as the wind picked up again. She began to walk, and as she did, the colours of her clothing shifted, red bleeding seamlessly to blue flowing easily to green. A new colour for each graceful step. Alex held his breath as she passed close by. Her floor-length gown brushed the ground with a soft, velvety swoosh.

He craned his head as far as his stone-stuck neck would let him. She was heading towards Pai's motionless body. And just like that, he knew.

Bastet.

The cat-headed goddess had been Alex's mom's favourite. He ran through everything he knew about her: a powerful goddess, revered by the ancient Egyptians as a protector of both the pharaoh and the people.

And he remembered the little information plaque they'd salvaged from Pai's wrecked case in London: PAI-EN-INMAR . . . FROM THE TEMPLE OF

BASTET... Cats were considered sacred in ancient Egypt because of their association with Bastet. And temple cats like Pai were the most sacred of all.

Bastet glided ever closer to her fallen servant.

To harm any cat was considered bad luck, thought Alex.

The goddess stood over Pai's twisted frame.

To harm a temple cat, well, that was just dumb...

Bastet bent down.

The Walker moved. Perhaps he had seen enough or perhaps he considered the cat's remains to be his now, part of his sacrificial offering. Perhaps he simply wanted a closer look. Whatever the reason, he took a step directly towards Pai – towards Bastet.

And it's never a good idea to challenge a goddess.

Her head turned and the slits of her cat eyes narrowed.

And she *changed*.

What had once been elegant and beautiful became fearsome. Her cat head was consumed by flames – red, then orange, then blue. Under the flames, Alex saw the shadow of her face, not a cat's now but a lioness's. Alex held his breath. Bastet was revered in ancient Egypt, but feared, too, and this was why. This was her other half. In her anger, she had taken on her predatory aspect. Standing before them now was her sister goddess. . .

Sekhmet.

The Destroyer.

Violence itself.

"Look away from her!" called Todtman.

Alex did as he was told. He looked instead towards the doomed Walker, who began to burn. The flames started at the edge of his ragged frame, and he writhed as they rushed inward, consuming him. Suddenly, his flaming body flew backwards across the pit. He hit the far wall at incredible speed, like a missile.

FWOOOOM!

Alex felt the impact through the stone surrounding him and closed his eyes against the advancing wall of pulverized stone.

Quiet moments passed and the dust settled.

"She is gone," breathed Todtman at last.

Alex opened his eyes and turned to look, surprised to find his neck no longer encased in stone but rather surrounded by powder. Slowly, he leaned forward and sat up. The powdered stone fell away, and he stood up, his limbs stiff but free. Todtman did the same, though the process was a bit harder on his old bones. Ren merely pulled her two feet free as if stepping out of a pair of stony slippers.

They all looked to the spot where Pai had been. The mummy cat was gone, and so was the one she served.

"Pai was just protecting me," said Ren, her voice both sad and unsure. "Do you think she's . . . dead?"

"She always was," said Todtman with characteristic bluntness.

Ren glared at Todtman, and then did a quick double take in that direction. "A way out!"

Alex followed her eyes. Now that the dust had settled, he saw a huge hole blown into the far wall. Behind it was a dark hollow space. "Sekhmet blasted the Death Walker right through the wall," said Alex, shaking his head. "That dude seriously picked the wrong cat to pick on."

"Pai saved us," said Ren.

Alex felt another quick stab of guilt: *Pai had saved them when he had failed, and it had cost her everything.* He felt the new burden settle atop all the others, and all he managed to say was a halfhearted "Yeah."

"No!" said Ren, insisting on it. "She. Saved. Us."

"Yes," said Todtman. "She sacrificed herself. She was noble – now let's get out of here!"

Todtman took four steps forward, two of them limps, but by his fifth step, Ren was under one arm, supporting him. By the sixth, Alex was under the other. They hurried through the gaping hole in the pit wall. There was no sign of the Walker, not so much as a rib or pale stone eye.

"You remember how you said that without the Lost Spells the Walkers might be able to come back again?" said Alex.

"Yes," said Todtman.

Alex took one more look around as they stepped through the smashed wall. "Well, I don't think this one is coming back."

Todtman smiled, but only briefly. As they stepped into the shadows, the finished floor and right angles told them this was not just a hole blasted into the rock. This was a room, and that meant this whole place was an underground stronghold.

"We must find a way out quickly," said Todtman. "The leader is here and possibly others – a small army of men and guns, at the least. This is not a fight we want right now."

Alex's mind flashed to the rogues' gallery of masked Order operatives they'd faced so far. But as they rushed across the room, it turned out it was the men and guns they had to deal with first. There were two of them, wearing the unmarked khaki uniforms The Order favoured.

As the guards saw them, their eyes widened and their hands went to the pistols at their belts. But Alex's hand was already on his scarab, and Todtman's on his falcon. A wicked wind shear shot from Alex's right hand. And his target was no ancient evil this time – this dude was maybe twenty-four. The wind slammed him backwards into the wall, and he slowly slid down it, stunned and gasping.

Todtman took a different approach. The jewelled eyes of the falcon glowed softly, and the eyes of the second guard glazed over. The Watcher exerted a powerful hold over weak minds, minds used to taking orders. The man slid his pistol back into its holster. Todtman pulled himself free from Alex and Ren and approached him.

"What is this place?" Todtman asked.

"It is a secure facility. The Death Walker protects it."

Alex nudged Ren. "Not any more."

"Protects what?" said Todtman. "What is here?"

The guard's subjugated brain seemed to search for the right English words. "The . . . stone warriors," he said at last. "And the prisoners."

Alex's eyes opened wide. *Had they caught his mom?*

Todtman was clearly thinking the same thing. "Americans?"

"One," said the guard.

Alex's heart stuttered. The first guard shifted on the floor and reached for his head, but Alex couldn't react. He needed to hear this.

Todtman pressed him. "A woman?"

The man looked confused for a moment and then shook his head. "Boy," he said.

Not his mom. Alex exhaled. Then something else occurred to him: *An American boy. . . Could it be Luke?* But the next moment he was chastising himself for being so stupid. He knew all too well that his super-jock cousin was working with The Order – probably getting ready to buy an NBA team with the money they must have paid him to betray them.

Alex saw movement out of the corner of his eye and turned just in time to see the first guard recover his bearings and reach for his gun. Alex spun around too late – but not Ren. She kicked the man hard in one bent shin.

The guard grabbed his shin and swore, giving Alex enough time to unleash a second blast of wind. The guard's head smacked back into the wall with a hollow coconut *BONK*, and he was knocked out cold. But no sooner had one threat ended than a larger one loomed. Voices echoed through the room, coming from somewhere out in the pit.

"We need to get out of here," said Ren.

Todtman nodded but didn't budge. "Where are these stone warriors?"

The guard resisted. Todtman clutched the falcon harder, leaned in and repeated himself in a hoarse, angry whisper: "WHERE?"

The guard raised his hand despite himself, pointing to a doorway along the half-shattered side wall. "One ... flight ... up ... to ... right," the man spat out, fighting himself on every word.

"One last thing," said Todtman, leaning back.

"We have to go," hissed Ren, the echoing voices louder now.

Alex gave her what he hoped was a reassuring look. "I'm sure it's important," he whispered.

"Do you have a broom?" asked Todtman. "It must get sandy in here..."

The guard looked confused but pointed to one shadowy corner. *"Vielen Dank,"* said Todtman. *Thank you very much.* "Now sleep."

The guard crumpled to the floor as Todtman hobbled to the corner.

"Let's go," he said as he used the falcon's power to shear off the head of the broom.

They rushed through the side door and up the stairs, one step ahead of the approaching voices. The only sounds were the soft, wooden thuds of Todtman's new walking stick.

ROCK STARS AND FAST CARS

The staircase led up and away from the shattered wall, and by the first landing, the electric lights were working again. "One flight up and to the right," Todtman repeated softly. "Here it is." He gestured towards a large, vaultlike door.

Alex was less interested in these "stone warriors," whatever that meant, and more interested in escape. "Why don't we keep going up the stairs?" he said as Ren nodded emphatically in agreement.

Todtman turned the large door handle. Locked.

He reached for his amulet. "We still know too little about The Order's plans," he said. "I must know what they are capable of, what tools they have. I saw something in Cairo, and it . . . troubled me."

Alex knew he had a point: The cult was up to something massive, and they needed to know more – not just what they planned to accomplish, but how. He took one last longing look up the stairwell and then turned his attention towards the door. Hand on amulet, Todtman's eyes slid closed and his augmented senses probed the inner workings of the lock, finding its weak point.

KLICKICK!

The lock opened, but still he searched.

CRECK!

The sound of a second, larger lock opening. . . *There's something important in there*, thought Alex. Todtman pushed the door open and stepped inside, Alex and Ren following a step behind.

The room was dark and Alex was on edge. He jumped when Todtman swung the heavy door shut behind them. Then he heard a third click, much softer this time, as the old scholar found the light switch.

Alex's breath caught and his heart nearly stopped.

His hand flew up to his amulet and he took a quick step back, nearly shouldering Ren into the wall. "Hey!" she said.

And then she saw it, too, and gasped sharply. Facing them were five massive, menacing figures. Menacing – and familiar.

They were in the shape of the five Order operatives who already haunted their nightmares. There was the treacherous, jackal-masked Al-Dab'u, their first adversary in New York; the cruel, crocodile-headed Ta-mesah from London; Peshwar, the sinister, lioness-skull-wearing huntress who'd pursued them halfway across Egypt; the vulture-veiled leader; and the grotesque Aff Neb.

But these were carved from blocks of rugged stone: ten feet tall and powerfully built, like Hulked-out versions of the sinister originals.

"The stone warriors are ... statues?" said Ren. "That's so *vain*!"

"No," said Todtman, his voice grave and fearful. "Not vain – terrifying. I was afraid of this. They hadn't taken shape yet in Cairo. I only saw a glimpse. But now. . ." He looked from Alex to Ren. "We must destroy these!"

"Why?" said Ren, but there was no time for

explanation, much less destruction. Behind them, the locks of the door were beginning to turn. The Order had caught up with them.

"We're trapped in here!" said Alex, surveying the featureless room.

"No," said Ren. "There has to be a back door."

"How do you know?" said Alex.

She rolled her eyes. "Because these things are too big to fit through the front one!"

The first lock had already clicked open and the larger second lock was beginning to turn. The friends rushed across the bare, echoing chamber, slaloming between the looming statues. They gave Alex a serious case of the creeps, a mix of bad memories and foreboding. *What are these things for – and why do they scare Todtman so much?*

They passed the last statue – the graven image of the cult leader – just as the door swung open and the man himself strode into the room. They reached the back wall. In its centre was the sort of large, rolling door you'd find on a loading dock.

"Phew!" said Ren.

"You two open it," said Todtman, turning back towards their pursuers. "I'll hold them off."

Alex looked at him like he was crazy. *How could*

he hold off the leader and the steady stream of armed men pouring in the door behind him? But there was no time for second thoughts.

"I'll unlock it," said Ren. "You push!"

Alex gave her a sceptical look, too. She had the least experience using an amulet – and this looked like a big lock. But she looked confident, and for the first time he realized that she had more faith in the ibis than he did.

He was plenty confident with his own amulet, though. He grasped the scarab, and once again the ancient energy coursed through him, quickening his pulse, sharpening his senses. He extended his right hand, palm up, and slowly raised it.

As he began to push, he saw a pop of white light and heard a muffled *klink*. Ren had done it! The big door began to move.

Behind them, Todtman's delay tactic was a masterstroke. Rather than attempt a direct attack on The Order forces, he threatened what they held dear. As the door rose to waist height, Alex risked a quick look back. The first of the statues, Al-Dab'u's, was wobbling and ... falling! The Order forces shouted in confusion and concern. "Stop it!" barked the leader. "Do not let it fall!"

Todtman's froggy face was red, his eyes protruding even more than usual from the effort of tipping the massive statue. But now gravity was on his side. The leader extended his own hand, pushing back, as half a dozen men rushed to prop the thing up. Behind them, Alex saw the pale skull of a lioness enter the room.

"Peshwar's here," he gasped.

"Let's go!" yelped Ren.

Todtman wheeled around, releasing the amulet with an exhausted gasp.

The three friends quickly ducked under the half-open gate as the room lit up red and one of Peshwar's energy daggers rocketed towards them. The deadly dagger slammed into the edge of the door as they straightened up on the other side.

"Glad I didn't have time to open it all the way!" said Alex.

Another advantage of the half-opened door: Closing it was much faster.

"Lock it!" said Todtman, already beginning to hobble across the broad concrete floor in front of them. "And break the lock!"

The same augmented senses and subtle manipulations that made it possible for Alex to open a lock with the scarab made it surprisingly easy to break off one of the small pieces inside.

He rushed to catch up with the others as a dozen hands began pounding on the stubbornly stuck metal behind them. The friends were in a large, bare room, its walls mostly lost in shadows. Up ahead, he could see a ramp sloping upward. It looked like an empty loading dock – but it wasn't empty.

"Hey, guys?" Alex heard. Just two words, but the voice was so familiar that he recognized it immediately. He wheeled around, reaching for his amulet once again. But the person he saw posed no threat this time. Pressed between thick iron bars along the far wall, a face floated like a ghost in the shadows.

"Luke?" The word flopped weakly out of Alex's mouth as he tried to come to terms with what he was seeing. He took a step forward and saw that there were three large doors along the far wall, each with a barred window in the centre. Luke was in the middle cell. *But why?* His cousin was working with The Order – wasn't he? Then why was he in a sunless cell in their desert citadel?

"You traitor!" shouted Ren. He'd betrayed her, too, but her tone softened as she stepped forward and got a better look at his pale, grime-streaked face. "You . . . snake?"

Luke managed a weak smile. "OK, I had that coming," he said. "But you gotta understand, I didn't want to do it. I mean, at first, yeah. The money was good, but then—"

Pa-KRACK! Ba-DOOOM!

Two quick, explosive sounds came through the door behind them, and two large bumps appeared on its metal surface.

Todtman peered into the gloom. "They are coming through. That door will not hold them much longer."

But Alex couldn't bring himself to leave just yet. Todtman had interacted with Luke only briefly, but Alex's cousin had been a big part of the team in London and the Valley of the Kings. His athletic ability and knack for saying the obvious had saved them more than once – even if he had been passing on information to The Order the whole time. Alex needed to hear this. "Why did you betray us?" he said.

Thin hands appeared on the bars of the other two cells, but the faces stayed hidden inside. For the first time, Alex caught a whiff of the stink coming from the cells. These people were being held in darkness and filth, and barely fed, by the looks of it.

"When I realized how bad these people really are," said Luke, "I couldn't do it any more."

"But you did!" yelled Ren. "You gave us away! We could have died!"

As if to punctuate her angry point, a third explosion rocked the door behind them. The metal began to give. Crimson light flickered through a long crack.

"I know," breathed Luke. "I feel terrible, but. . ."

"WE HAVE TO GO!" shouted Todtman.

Alex looked at his cousin closely. He *had* betrayed them. They'd survived it out in the desert, but if he kept them here any longer this time, he'd deliver them into the hands of The Order agents – whether he meant to or not.

"I'm sorry, man," he said, and turned to run. Sympathy and old loyalty tugged at him, but he pulled away. They didn't have time to listen to Luke's excuses.

Ren followed half a step behind. They'd already reached the ramp and started up it when Luke called out his last words. "They were going to kill my parents! I'm sorry, cuz!"

Alex wheeled around and stared back down into the darkness. An image formed in his head, one perfectly suited to this shadowy place. Once again, he pictured that complex spiderweb. Back in Alexandria, he'd imagined his mom was the centre, but really he was the spider. This was all his fault, and not just on some big, abstract level, but right down to each person involved.

Luke had got pulled into that web because of Alex. He never would've betrayed them in a million years if it weren't for the lure of money and the worst threat imaginable. Luke's drained face watched him through the gloom, a glimmer of hope shining through now.

Hardly believing his own words, Alex heard himself say, "I have to save him."

He turned and took a step back down the ramp, once again heading towards danger, but quick footsteps came up behind him.

"No, Ren, don't—" he began, just as a burst of crimson light blew a massive hole in the metal gate. *Fa-THOOOM!*

In the quiet following the explosion, Ren made it crystal clear that she had no intention of following his suicide mission. She reached up and slapped the swollen lump on the back of his head. Alex winced as if he'd just bitten down on a lemon, and sucked air through his teeth. "OW!"

"Listen to me!" she said. "I don't know what this cowboy craziness is all about, but if you don't turn around right now, we are *all* going to end up in that cell – or worse."

"But it's all my—" Alex began, but Ren cut him short.

"It is not!"

Alex heard the metal gate begin to roll upward and the angry voices massing behind it. He was paralysed. He felt responsible for all of them, but saving one meant putting the others in danger.

It was Luke himself who broke the deadlock: "Go, man!" he shouted. "Just go!"

Alex released a wordless shout of frustration and anger – but he went. He took one last look back at Luke's face and then rushed towards Todtman, who was using his amulet to try to slow the rising gate.

Ren added a blinding flash to the delay tactics, and then they all turned and rushed up the ramp towards freedom. By the time the battered gate rattled fully open behind them, Todtman was already opening the next gate with his amulet. They hurried through, the slap of footsteps and crackle of energy close behind. Sunlight and dry desert air met them on the other side.

As Todtman and Ren closed the gate and broke the lock, two gunshots pushed little cones into the metal from the other side. Alex stared at them, understanding that if he'd hesitated even a few seconds longer, those bullets might be lodged in his back – or his friend's.

"Our getaway!" called Ren, pointing.

A small fleet of expensive new cars sat in a square lot, all in identical gunmetal grey. Even with sun-stung eyes Alex could make out the familiar logo. Mercedes-Benzes.

"Ausgezeichnet!" shouted Todtman. *Excellent!*

They hustled towards the nearest one. "Can you start it?" asked Ren as Todtman slid into the driver's seat.

"Of course!" Todtman said, grabbing his amulet. "These cars make perfect sense – they're German!"

The powerful engine roared to life, and they burned rubber leaving the lot.

Alex took one last look behind them as the car hit the long ribbon of hot asphalt that would lead them to safety. He stared at The Order's subterranean stronghold... Sand-coloured canvas had already been drawn over the top of the shattered pit. The pit where they had lost Pai, and nearly each other, before encountering a goddess. The gate they'd come through was just beginning to slide open again. And somewhere behind them, his cousin, held captive and caught in the crossfire of all this, his life or death dependent on the whims of maniacs.

Finally, he allowed himself to look at the road ahead, but he didn't really see it. What he saw instead was a spiderweb. He looked down at himself, turned his hand over and considered it. He was the spider. And he was *poisonous*.

As the luxury sedan's air conditioning kicked in, he took his first deep breath of cool air in what felt like ages. He filled his lungs with air and his mind with one single word, the only thing that could make this all worth it. The only thing that could tear the web apart and release everyone who'd been caught up in it.

Minyahur.

TO MINYAHUR

Todtman punched their destination into the navigation system, shifted the powerful sedan into gear, and pressed the gas pedal to the floor. Alex settled into the back seat, not noticing the fat black fly crawling slowly along the edge of the door.

The Mercedes sped south as the sun began to set in the west. Todtman took them through a few small towns and made a series of seemingly random turns, in case they were being followed. But Alex saw no suspicious cars tailing them, and the sleek vehicle seemed like a safe haven: a little bubble of tinted glass and air conditioning.

For a while, nobody said very much. They were too tired and all working through what had just happened in their own ways. Alex couldn't see Ren's small frame on the other side of the big front seat, but he heard her sniffle a few times and knew it was about Pai.

But eventually they recovered, like boxers picking themselves up off the mat, and the need to make sense of what they'd seen was too strong for silence.

Ren had been trying to puzzle something out herself for about thirty miles, and now she was just going to ask Todtman. "What was the big deal about those statues?" she said. "Why were you so – I mean, no offence, but why were you so freaked out about them?"

"They are powerful and dangerous weapons. I dearly wish we'd had time to destroy them."

"Dangerous?" said Ren. "What's The Order going to do, hit people with them? They can't even move."

"Not yet," said Todtman. At first, she thought he was joking, but the grim look on his face didn't crack, just deepened. "You already know that the ancient Egyptians believed they could make a statue of themselves in life and inhabit that form in the afterlife..."

"Right," said Ren, remembering. "Like in London, the second Death Walker, Willoughby... He looked just like the statue in his crypt."

"And King Tut looked just like his famous mask," added Alex.

Ren was happy to recall the sight of Tutankhamun in the Valley of the Kings, looking less like a boy king and more like a member of a boy band. "Yeah," she confirmed. "He was supercute."

"I will take your word for it," said Todtman. "But these statues were not made for their looks. They were made to be warriors."

"So wait," said Alex, "The Order guys want to 'inhabit' those forms? They want to be ten feet tall and made of stone?"

"They want to be invulnerable to harm," said Todtman. "Unstoppable."

"But wouldn't they need to be dead first? Like Tut and Willoughby?"

Todtman took his eyes off the road and turned back towards Alex in a way that made Ren fear for her own life. "And you don't think they would do that?" he said sharply. "The Order—"

"Is a death cult," she said. "We know. Could you please keep your eyes on the road?" But then she finally understood the full implication of what he was saying. "So wait, they plan to sacrifice themselves? They plan to turn *themselves* into Death Walkers?"

Alex groaned. "Into supersized, indestructible Death Walkers."

HONK!

An approaching truck finally caught Todtman's attention – with its horn rather than its grille, thankfully. He veered back into his lane. "And I suspect their powers would be just as large as their bodies," he said. "The Lost Spells unleashed the Death Walkers into this world, and the Lost Spells would allow these new ones to cross over, as well. And with the protection of those Spells. . ."

"They would be impossible to banish, brought back for good," said Alex. Ren turned and saw him looking down at his scarab. "The Book of the Dead, the scarab, nothing could stop them."

Ren tried to imagine it. Supersized Death Walkers with supersized powers. "Can you imagine how powerful Peshwar would be?" she said. "Those

163

energy daggers could take down a building! Or their leader? Oh wow. . ."

"He could control presidents, nations," said Todtman. "And nothing could stop them – or even harm them."

"No wonder they're working with the Death Walkers," said Alex. "They are planning to *become* Death Walkers."

Todtman nodded solemnly. "The world of the dead is already bleeding into the world of the living, already taking hold. The Order and the Death Walkers plan to use that opening to rule – to live for ever and rule a world shadowed by death."

Ren sat back, trying to imagine a world ruled by The Order and the Death Walkers. It was not a world she wanted any part of. "It's a good thing we're on our way to find the Spells right now," she said. "We need to slam those doorways shut and put everything back the way it was!"

She looked at the other two. Todtman was nodding, but Alex. . . Alex looked like she'd just punched him. She didn't understand his reaction at all, at first. And then she did. "Oh," she said. "Oh no."

Todtman kept his eyes fixed on the road. "Yes,"

he said. "We have no way of knowing what will happen if the doorways close for good, but the risk was always clear – the risk to Alex."

Always clear? she thought. *Clear to who?* She hadn't signed up for this.

"Was it clear to you?" she said, staring back between the seats at Alex and not entirely succeeding in keeping the pity out of her voice.

"I was kind of trying not to think about it," he admitted. "But if we use the Spells and everything goes back to the way it was before, well. . ."

He couldn't bring himself to say it, and she didn't blame him.

Because he was sick before – sick, at best.

At worst, he was dead.

That night, with the sun gone red again and just kissing the horizon, they arrived in Minyahur.

A LAND OF SAND AND SECRETS

Alex climbed out of the car into what felt like a different world, one where stone monsters were waiting to be born and where winning the battle against them might mean losing his life. He looked around as the others stood and stretched beside him. The little village was locked up as tight as a bank vault. It wasn't even nine o'clock yet, but the half dozen buildings that made up the centre of town slumbered like huddled animals. The doors were locked and the windows were dark and shuttered.

The only light came from the rising moon and one lone streetlight.

This was Minyahur, the place his mom thought of as a sanctuary, a quiet shelter in a mad world. The place he hoped to find her now.

"Well, at least they have electricity," Ren said, stretching her legs and gazing up at the flickering bulb.

There wasn't much for the faint light to reveal: A sandy landscape stretched out into the darkness. Lopsided mud-brick huts slumped together in modest bunches, with squared-off redbrick structures scattered among them like dropped Monopoly houses. Even the most run-down buildings seemed to have heavy doors and thick wooden shutters on the windows. *Are there lights burning behind those shutters?* he wondered. *Is the town asleep, or is everyone gone?*

"Not very welcoming," said Ren, looking around sceptically.

Alex removed his scarab from under his shirt. It felt hot in his hand. Whatever the fate of the villagers, he now knew this: *The dead are walking here.*

"Why don't you two start looking around?" said Todtman. "I will try to find us somewhere to stay."

Ren looked at the dark, quiet buildings, each one as silent and still as a gravestone. "What if something has happened to them all?"

"Exactly," said Todtman. "We need to make sure that everything is all right here, that we will be safe for the night. But don't go far."

Alex and Ren watched him turn and head towards the street, his broomstick cane making soft stabbing sounds as it punched into the sandy ground.

"Come on," said Alex. "There are some more buildings over this way."

They started out along the road, but it felt too exposed and without a word they veered off into the soft sand alongside. Wearing the boots he'd broken in in the Valley of the Kings, he felt at home in the sand. Boots just like his mom had always worn on her work expeditions.

For the first time in what felt like for ever, it seemed not just possible but likely that she was nearby. The familiar anticipation stirred inside him. He looked around at the desolate village: It looked like she had run to the very ends of the earth to escape them. To escape *him*. And this time, he didn't really blame her. *Who wouldn't run from a spider?*

They headed deeper into the village's sandy outskirts. One direction, Alex knew, led to the Nile – the source and anchor of all life in Egypt, rolling slowly north somewhere just beyond his sight. The other led farther into the vast Sahara desert. He looked out at it. The sand glowed like endless snow in the moonlight. It was beautiful, but he needed more than his eyes could give him now. He reached up and wrapped his hand around his amulet. His pulse quickened and his breath caught as he felt the exhilarating rush of ancient energy crackle through his system.

Suddenly, the world around him began to shimmer ever so slightly. He'd hoped he could use the scarab to pinpoint a single strong signal. Instead, the living dead – or the death magic that brought them back – seemed to be all around them.

"Not good," he said, letting the scarab go. Using it for too long gave him a headache, anyway.

They were approaching a little hut made of mud bricks, and Alex wasn't sure if they should avoid it or check for signs of life. Up close, he could see that it was painted a mustard yellow that seemed oddly cheerful. As he eyed it, he saw a ragged figure pull itself from the dark side of the house and out into the open. "Ren!" he said, but she'd already seen it.

They both reached for their amulets with gunfighter speed.

The figure stepped clear of the house and out into the moonlight. It was a raggedly dressed old man. Ren let out a deep breath and Alex felt his shoulders relax. But neither of them let go of their amulets as the old beggar began to speak.

"Ah, children, strange children," he said.

Alex looked at the man. His skin was leathery and his hair was a matted and windblown mess. His frame was extremely thin and covered in an old brown robe. Alex hadn't expected khakis or anything, but a ratty robe? They really were in the middle of nowhere now.

Alex took a deep breath and plastered on a smile. "We're looking for someone," he said.

"Oh yes? And who might that be?"

"A woman," he said. "A foreigner."

"I think I might know something about that," said the old man enigmatically.

"Alex!" hissed Ren, taking a step back.

But Alex ignored her, taking a step forward. *Does this old man really know something about my mom?*

"I'll tell you," the man said. "For a coin."

Alex reached into his pocket.

"Alex!" said Ren, louder this time.

He shot her a look: *Not now!* With his hand still on his amulet, he felt safe. He pulled a handful of Egyptian coins out of his pocket. The man extended his hand, long nails pointing out, his palm creased with dirt. But as Alex dropped the coins into the man's hand, something occurred to him. *How can I understand this man? What are the odds that a beggar on the fringes of Arabic-speaking Egypt speaks perfect English?* As the change began to fall, he looked down at his amulet – the one that allowed him to speak ancient Egyptian when he held it. *Uh-oh.*

The change hit the man's greasy palm – and fell right through it. The coins thunked softly into the sand below.

The old man – or his spirit, anyway – looked down at the fallen coins and then looked up at Alex with a sheepish grin. "I never was very good with money," he said. And as he did, he began to change. His mouth widened, his eyes went black in the moonlight. . .

Alex scrambled back and felt his foot catch on a stone. He windmilled his arms for balance but it was too late. He hit the ground hard enough to feel a sharp pain shoot up his tailbone into his spine. He looked up and saw a ring of sharp teeth with a pure blackness at its centre. His hand had come off his amulet in the fall, and he fumbled for it desperately.

FWOOOP!

A blinding white flash lit his vision, leaving him seeing stars and nothing else. He rolled away blindly, the gritty sand rubbing against his skin and slipping into his clothing.

When his vision cleared, he looked up to see the teeth replaced by . . . Ren.

"If I am going to keep saving your butt," she said, "the least you can do is stop falling on it."

"Yeah, ha-ha," said Alex, extending his hand and attempting to salvage at least a little of his dignity. "If you're going to keep blinding me with that thing, the least you could do is help me up."

Ren reached down and took his outstretched hand. "I think we should probably head back now," she said, giving him a tug.

"Yeah, good idea," said Alex, eyeing a desert that suddenly looked less beautiful than eerie.

They walked back wordlessly. Alone with his thoughts, Alex finally allowed himself to really think about what Todtman had said: *"The risk was always clear."* A risk. . . Not a certainty.

And what exactly was the risk? He could deal with being sick again, though he would dearly miss this new health. He stood up straight and breathed in the clear desert air. He felt his system working smoothly and efficiently: extracting oxygen, pumping blood. There was no needles-and-pins stinging in his limbs, no bowling-ball queasiness in his gut, no lead-heavy exhaustion. He'd got so used to this, almost took it for granted now. Yeah, he'd miss it. But it was the other possibility that he needed to face: *Will this mission cost me my life? Or is there some way we could end The Order's plans without ending* me, *too?*

The truth was, he didn't know, and that's what he needed to make peace with. He listened to the muffled crunch of his best friend's footsteps and stared up at a moon as pale as bone. He'd caused so much trouble to so many people already. Maybe this was the way it had to be. Ren had been risking her own safety for him this whole time. Maybe it was time for him to take the biggest risk of all, for her – and everyone else.

He glanced over at his friend, her small frame

dwarfed by a barren desert that stretched to the horizon. He felt as if he had dragged her to the end of the earth, too, put her through so much. *Am I willing to die to end all this?* he wondered.

He kicked the ground and walked on.

I should be dead already.

CALLED OUT

Todtman had found them a place to stay, all right –
right back in the Benz. "There are people here," he had
said. "But they are afraid. I think, perhaps, it is best
not to impose on them right now – or to trust them."

An hour later, Ren was lying in the back seat,
since she was short enough to fit. The other two had
the front seats reclined as far as they would go. She
looked out the wide rear window at the sky above. It
was so dense with stars that it seemed to shimmer
and pulse. It didn't press down on her vision as

much as lift it up. They were still parked behind the same little cluster of buildings. *Are we safe here?* she wondered.

A car, when it came right down to it, didn't offer much shelter. And yet, she didn't feel afraid. Part of that was her company. Todtman was formidable with his falcon – even if he was snoring a little too loudly at present. And sometimes it seemed like Alex could move mountains with that scarab. *Amazing for a kid who couldn't even get through gym class a year ago. . .* But part of it had nothing to do with the others. She looked down to see the ibis glowing softly in the starlight.

She considered it again with fresh eyes. She could do so much more with it now. She could pick locks and zap spirits and blind the occasional giant fly. And as for the images, maybe she had just been thinking about them the wrong way. She'd always thought that it was giving her answers and she was failing to understand them half the time. But what if it was just giving her information, guidance? *What if it isn't the answer key? What if it is the studying?*

Alone in the back seat, she smiled. More than anyone else she knew, she liked studying.

A moment later, she was snoring, too.

*

The next morning dawned sunny, despite it all.

Alex woke up first, seat-sore and hungry. His body felt creaky, but inside he was buzzing. If this was the day they finally found his mom, it could be the best day of his life. It could also be the last. It felt like Christmas morning, with maybe a little too much Halloween thrown in. He tried to imagine seeing her again, after so long. *Would I run up and hug her?* he wondered. *Would she let me?*

He twisted his stiff neck towards the back seat. "Hey, Ren," he said over the sound of Todtman's precise, measured snoring. "You awake?"

"I am now," she groaned.

The exchange woke Todtman. *"Guten Morgen,"* he croaked.

Alex and Ren responded with grunts.

Donk! Donk! Donk!

All three heads whipped around. There was a man outside the car, knocking on Todtman's window. Todtman straightened his seat and lowered the window. There was a quick conversation in Arabic, a few bills handed over, and the man vanished.

"That is the owner of the store we are parked behind," said Todtman. "There is a fee for parking here. I suspect it has been in effect for exactly as long as we have been here. Also, he wanted to know if we want breakfast."

"Definitely," said Alex. His feelings were a confusing swirl, but his stomach was making itself very clear by rumbling loudly.

The three climbed out of Hotel Mercedes and into the bright Egyptian daylight. They walked around the buildings and on to the main road, doing their best to stretch and smash down their Benz-head hair as they went.

Alex was surprised by the number of people on the street. Minyahur had been a ghost town the night before – literally – but now it was alive with activity. He checked the time on his phone. Apparently, the village that shuts down early wakes up early, too. Looking at the heavy wooden shutters, flung open now, he thought he understood. Ren had saved him from a terrifying fate with her ibis last night, but these people didn't have amulets. They had only solid walls to hide behind.

He heard footsteps and stepped aside as a group of women walked past on the cracked concrete sidewalk. They were wearing traditional Muslim garb, covered head-to-toe in long black abayas and veils that left only their eyes visible.

"Aren't they hot?" whispered Ren as they passed, looking down at her own sporty, short-sleeved outfit.

Alex scanned the village centre. There were dozens of people, carrying bags or leading children or just walking swiftly towards some unknown destination. Most of the men wore pumpkin-sized turbans and the traditional white Egyptian gowns known as *galabeyas*. But almost all the women were wearing those same all-concealing black outfits. *It's a perfect disguise*, he realized with both horror and some small bit of admiration. *Mom could walk right past me and I'd never know.*

A bell tinkled as they pushed through the front door of the store.

"Ah!" said the shopkeeper. "Breakfast, yes?" He gave Alex and Ren a quick look and a slick smile. "How is my English? Good, yes? It used to be, but I do not get a chance to practise much out of here."

Alex smiled back politely. "So," he said. "What kind of breakfast are we talking about?"

It was mostly dry, sugary biscuits and tea, but they all wolfed it down at a small table in the back of the store. Then they headed towards the front to pay for the food – and extra for any information.

"The shopkeepers hear everything in a town like this," whispered Todtman.

But if this man had heard everything, he said nothing. *A foreign woman?* Not that he was aware of. *Any outsiders at all?* Couldn't think of any. *Anything out of the ordinary lately?* Ghosts and disappearances; rumours of a mummy. Nothing living.

They paid for the meal, a bottle of water, a can of insect repellant, and a cheap backpack, since Alex's and Ren's were still somewhere back in The Order's secret citadel. Alex put the stuff in the pack and the pack on his back and headed towards the door. But that's when he spotted something on a middle shelf: a quick flash of a familiar colour. He turned back to the shopkeeper.

"This tea here, with the purple label," he said. "Do you sell a lot of it?"

The man looked up at the tea and then back down at the cash register. "Not much," he said. "It was a special order. Most people around here prefer the Egyptian—" He tensed visibly and swallowed the next word. After what seemed to Alex a very deliberate pause, he continued. "It is neither our most popular brand nor our least. Have a nice day! If you are still around tonight, we also serve dinner."

He slammed the cash register shut, and with it, the conversation.

Alex tapped the metal tea canister. The little bonk he got back told him two things. First, the container was half empty. Second, his mother knew Egypt well – but he knew her better than anyone.

20

THE BUZZ AROUND TOWN

"She's here!" said Alex as they stepped out into the bright, hot morning. "In Minyahur! He sold her tea – he special ordered it for her!"

Ren swatted at one of the many flies buzzing dizzily around the centre of town. "How can we get him to tell us where she is?"

"That, he will not know," said Todtman. "She will come in at irregular times, he will say, unpredictable. She will pay in cash and leave quietly, maybe slip out while he is talking to another customer. Sometimes she will head in one direction, sometimes she will head in another."

"How do you know any of that?" said Ren.

"Because that is what I would do," Todtman said simply. "We must search the edges of the village. She would not stay in its centre."

They stood on the edge of the sidewalk, waiting to cross the street. There were no cars in sight, but a passing donkey cart was in no hurry.

"Why didn't she buy the whole container of tea," Alex asked Todtman as they reached the other side, "instead of leaving half of it there for me to see?"

"Maybe she did and the storekeeper bought another, hoping for more business," said Todtman with a shrug. "Or maybe she couldn't afford it."

The thought of his mom counting coins and buying only as much tea as she could hit Alex like a punch in the gut. He imagined her eating half of one of those chalky biscuits for lunch, saving the other for dinner. *Hungry, and on her own...*

"Ow!" he said, slapping down hard at his neck.

"Yes," said Todtman. "Sand flies. Nasty little beasts – and maybe worse. I think it's time for that insect repellant."

And maybe worse... Alex was thinking the same

thing: *Could these flies be spies, too?* Alex removed the spray can from his pack, and Ren plucked it from his hands.

"This looks like it's from World War Two," she said, scrutinizing the peeling label on the unpainted steel can. "Half the ingredients are probably banned in the US."

But they took turns spraying themselves. Alex coated his arms and neck and Ren applied it in small puffs, like perfume. Todtman, who had long sleeves, coated his hands and face.

They resumed their search, heading away from the centre of town.

"I'll try my amulet again," said Alex, reaching up and pulling it out from underneath his shirt. He stopped, closed his eyes, and grasped the scarab. The night before he'd sensed a diffuse signal spread across the landscape – death magic everywhere. But something had changed. Alex suddenly felt like he was holding a baked potato fresh from the oven. The sensitive flesh of his palm sizzled, and his vision lit up from the inside in red and orange and gold.

He gasped and dropped the scalding scarab.

He opened his eyes. Colour still swirled at the

edges of his vision as he looked down at his palm. No physical burns or blisters that he could see.

"What is it?" said Ren, clearly picking up the shock and pain in his expression.

Alex looked at his best friend, who was wreathed in stars.

"It's the Lost Spells," he managed. "They're here."

"Did you get a direction?" said Todtman.

Alex looked at him, his vision just now beginning to clear, and answered as best he could.

"No – I couldn't tell. It was too intense. But they're close," he said. "Very close."

"That is good," said Todtman, "because I think we are about to have company."

At first, Alex didn't understand what he meant, but as the swirling colours subsided, his vision continued to shift and buzz. He looked all around. The villagers were gone, hanging back from the three visitors. In their place, a sea of flies. Vicious little sand flies buzzed in clouds in the air, and every flat surface within twenty feet was dotted with big black flies.

"Uh-oh," said Alex, and as he did, a fat black fly darted inside his mouth like a filthy drop of midnight.

21

WHERE IN THE WORLD IS MAGGIE BAUER?

Alex gagged and spit out the fly. It hit the ground like a wet pellet.

"We're in trouble," he said. "Aff Neb is here." He wiped his forearm across his mouth, spat again.

Todtman looked around at the buzzing, crawling swarm. "Yes, or he will be soon. I think they are watching us for him. He will be powerful out here among so many . . . friends. And I doubt he will be alone."

The Order had endless firepower. Alex feared Peshwar and their leader – not to mention a small army of hired guns – were also nearby. *Had they just led an unstoppable force straight to his mom and the Spells?*

His head buzzed inside and out. Flies swarmed around him, one biting his neck while another got tangled in his hair. He felt angry and frustrated – but not helpless. "Hold on to something," he said through gritted teeth.

The wind began behind them and rolled towards them through the wide streets of the little village. It brought with it a wall of roiling sand. The Fly Lord would be powerful out here, but he wasn't the only one with desert magic. The familiar mantra formed in Alex's head. *The wind that comes before the rain...*

Alex spread his stance wide and let that wind roll over him. Ren grabbed on to the post of a nearby fence. Todtman speared his walking stick into the ground and leaned forward into it, forming a tripod.

The flies lacked such options.

For a few moments, the whipping wind drowned out all sound and the rolling sand cloud blocked out the sun. When it passed, the air was clear and the flies were gone. Villagers who had ducked into huts and alleyways for shelter began gophering their heads back out for a look.

"That is better," said Todtman, coughing up a little sand. "But it won't hold them for long – nor will it delay their master."

Alex nodded. "We need to find my mom *now*." Without another word, both Alex and Todtman turned and looked at Ren. "You must use the ibis," said Todtman. "We don't have time to argue."

But Alex stayed silent. He'd noticed something about Ren lately. She was less hesitant with her amulet, less unsure, more...

"Ready!" she said, folding her hand around the ibis.

Ren closed her eyes.

A moment later, her eyes fluttered open.

"What did you see?" said Alex, leaning towards her expectantly.

"Same as last time," she said. "Nothing at all."

Alex kicked the ground hard in frustration.

"Well, that is no help," said Todtman, turning away.

"No, wait," said Ren. "You're thinking about it wrong. It doesn't give answers, just information." She turned to Todtman. "Last time I saw nothing you said it meant the Spells were being hidden or protected by some kind of magic."

"Yes," he said. "So?"

"So, they're hidden again," said Ren. She pointed at Alex. "But they weren't when he tried it last time – their signal nearly burned his hand off."

"That's true," Alex admitted. "That hurt."

"Do it again," said Ren.

"What? No way!" he said.

Ren broke into the smallest of smiles and then, imitating Todtman's accent, she said: "We don't have time to argue."

Well, she's got me there, thought Alex. His hand closed around the scarab. He closed his eyes and reached out with his senses, steeling himself for the burning pain and shock to come. Instead...

"Nothing," he said. "Just the same little shimmer I got last night. Weak, and all around." He turned towards Todtman. "What does it mean?"

"The Spells were unprotected, briefly," he said. "She must have had them out in the open, and now she has hidden them again... Perhaps she has seen the flies, too."

"Or the windstorm," said Alex. "She'd recognize that. This used to be her amulet."

"Either way, we know the Spells are nearby, and they have been concealed again," said Todtman.

"So she's here, and she's watching," said Alex, suddenly looking all around.

"Perhaps getting her attention is not the worst thing now," said Todtman. "We have no more time to waste – and nothing left to lose."

"But why get her attention?" said Ren. "She's hiding from us."

"Hiding, yes," said Todtman. "But also *protecting* the Spells. If there's a threat to them..."

"She'd want to know," Alex chimed in, picking up the thought.

"Tell me," said Todtman. "If you saw your mother – even disguised, covered head to toe – do you think you could recognize her?"

Alex thought about it. He considered the million multifaceted memories that made up their history together. He remembered his mom sitting quietly across the kitchen table from him, him half-playing a game on the iPad, her half-reading some thick book, how sometimes they'd both look up at each other at exactly the same moment – who knows why – smile, and look down again.

"Yeah," he said. "I think so."

"Good," said Todtman. "Then we must use the amulets again."

"Which one of us?" said Ren.

Todtman smiled. "All of us, of course."

"On the count of three," said Todtman. "One, two. . ."

They all reached for their amulets. The Order was on the way, and Alex knew they would not be subtle in finding his mom. They would burn this little village to the ground and tear the veils from people's faces. The three Amulet Keepers wouldn't resort to such tactics, but this was clearly no time for half measures.

"Three!"

Alex closed his left hand around the scarab. As soon as he felt the ancient energy crackle through his veins, he began waving his right hand above him in a little circle, like a cowboy twirling a lasso. A whipping, swirling wind kicked up and immediately began picking up the sand that lay all around them in the little desert outpost. A whooshing sound filled the streets, and a tall funnel appeared, the circular air currents made visible as walls of whirling sand.

The people on the street turned to look as the sand devil towered ever higher. Others stepped out of doors or poked their heads out of windows for a closer look. Sand augers and dust whirls were common out here – but not like this.

"Now, Ren!" called Todtman through the whipping maelstrom that now surrounded them.

Ren clutched the ibis tighter and thrust her free hand straight upward.

FWOOP!

A flash of brilliant white light lit up the sky, reflecting off millions of shiny sand crystals. A beautiful wash of splintered white light carried to the very edges of the village.

Alex heard gasps and shouts from the gathering crowd. More eyes turned to the spectacle, and more feet carried them towards it. Finally, Todtman did his part. Alex had seen him use the Watcher to control individual minds many times, but now he needed more than that. He squeezed the stone falcon tight and shouted: "Watch! Look!"

The sound of his voice was all but drowned out by the whipping wind, but his psychic cry carried across the desert. The few doors that had remained closed were flung open now. Suddenly, even the most cautious villager felt the strong desire to see this towering but harmless twister.

Ren lit it with another flash – *FWOOP!* – and the *oooh*s and *aah*s came from a much larger crowd.

Alex's head was beginning to pound and his arm was starting to tire.

"Enough!" called Todtman.

Alex released the scarab and let his aching arm drop. The column of swirling sand collapsed straight down.

"Ack!" called Ren, covering her head.

But the wind had stopped so abruptly that most of the sand fell heavily in a circle all around the friends, leaving them standing inside a sloping foxhole nearly two feet high.

"Look quickly!" called Todtman. "She will be at the edges. The Watcher will not hold a mind like hers. She will stay no longer than is necessary to identify the threat. . ."

Alex scanned the edge of the crowd furiously. There were scores of people now, the entire population of the little village. Most of them stood and pointed and conferred nervously with their neighbours. Alex got the distinct impression that they were no strangers to magic out here. He turned in a circle. The people closest to him blocked his view of those on the edges of the crowd – many of whom were already beginning to leave. The women vexed him in their all-concealing garb. *Why can't I have thousands of lenses in my eyes like Aff Neb?* he wondered desperately.

The crowd continued to disperse, having already sized up these amulet-bearing newcomers.

I'm losing my chance, thought Alex. He needed to concentrate and so he ignored the eyes of the women, ignored their shoulders and walks and any of the other markers he thought he might be able to identify. Instead, he concentrated on just one thing.

He turned and turned and craned his neck around those who remained. And just when he thought he would collapse from dizziness and desperation and one breath held way too long, he saw something.

"There!" he said as the woman disappeared down a side alley thirty yards away.

"Where?" called Ren. "Which one?"

Alex scrambled over the sloping wall of sand in front of him and took off running. He had barely got a look at her, and that was fine, because there wasn't much to see. Mostly just a flash of plain black abaya, indistinguishable from two dozen others on the street.

But he *had* seen something. And as soon as he

had, any reservations he'd harboured about finding his mom melted away like mist in the desert sun. He picked up speed as he dodged and ducked his way through the crowd, scaring people as he ran up behind them, and leaving his friends in the dust.

An arm reached for him as he ran through the scattering throng, and another, alarmingly, grabbed at his amulet. He shouldered through the first and slapped aside the second. He kept his eyes trained on the approaching alleyway, not even daring to spare a glare for the would-be thief.

"Mom!" he called, his eager voice breaking. "Mom!"

He hit the alleyway too fast and crashed into the far wall before he could turn. He used the impact to bounce himself back in the right direction without missing a beat. He was in a narrow space between two of the village's larger buildings, and at the very end of that space, walking briskly, was a woman in black.

Once she reached the end, she could turn in either direction. Then she could find the next alley and do the same. As small as the village was, Alex had no doubt that she knew it well enough to escape him.

He looked down to avoid a garbage can lid and when he looked up, the woman was gone.

Stupid, he thought. *So stupid.*

He called out again, desperation dripping from his voice now: "Mom!"

He had found her and lost her, and now she knew he was on her trail. Now she could escape again. He'd travelled thousands of miles, only to fall a few yards short. He called out one final time as he neared the end of the alley. And this time there was more than desperation in it. There was sadness, the breaking voice of a broken heart.

And maybe that's why. . .

Because he expected to find nothing as he reached the end of the alley, but that was not the case.

A woman stood with her back to him, halfway to the next alley. Her head was covered in black cloth, but he knew who it was immediately.

"Mom?" he said.

The woman turned and removed her head-covering niqab.

And for the first time in what felt like a lifetime, Alex Sennefer saw his mom. All his doubts – did she still love him, was she mad at him for what he'd cost

196

her – melted away at the simple fact of her presence. After weeks of living in tight-chested anxiety, as if at every point he'd taken one breath too few, his lungs filled with one long, relieved breath.

There was a tear carving a dark path through the dust on his mom's cheek, and it trembled and fell as she opened her mouth to speak. "I couldn't run from you," she said. "Not any more. I couldn't hear your voice and run."

Alex opened his mouth but nothing came out.

"How did you know it was me?" she said, giving him a simple prompt, once again making his life easier.

Alex noticed some new grey in her hair, which managed to be both tightly bundled and utterly disheveled. Then he looked down and pointed. He didn't know if his voice would work until it did.

"I recognized your boots."

22

A DOOR IN THE FLOOR

It definitely wasn't the first time Ren turned a corner to find Alex hugging his mom. Back when Alex was a sick only-child and Dr Bauer was a hardworking single mom, they often hugged before going their separate ways. Towards the end of his life – his first life – they'd hugged a little longer, never quite sure if they'd see each other again.

Ren gave them their space as they hugged hard, with their eyes closed to the world. She was pretty sure they didn't even realize she was there. They were lost in the reunion and defenceless. And suddenly she felt intensely protective of them. Her left hand drifted towards her amulet. She would watch the hostile world for them.

But as she turned one way and then another, she couldn't help but think of her own parents. She remembered her own goodbye hugs at the airport. It felt so long ago now. *Too long.* Her watchful eyes began to brim with tears, and as protective as she felt, she couldn't help but feel a tiny bit jealous, too.

And so when Todtman pivoted around the corner on the tip of his cane, she didn't try to stop him. She knew him well enough by now to know what he would do.

The old curator took in the moment at a glance, paused barely half a beat, and said, "Maggie!"

Dr Bauer gave her son one more squeeze and closed her eyes a little tighter, as if trying to lock in the moment. Then she opened them and looked over her son's shoulder.

"*Guten Tag*, Ernst," she said, and then, more softly, "Hello, Ren. It's good to see you."

Ren felt her ears get hot – embarrassed to be caught staring – and offered a quick wave.

"The Order is on its way," said Todtman, by way of hello. "They may already be here."

Maggie sighed heavily and nodded. Then she released her son and looked down at him. Alex looked up at her, his arms still held out for a hug that was now over. "Did you do that sand devil?" she said, eyeing the scarab that had once been hers.

Alex nodded.

She reached down and ruffled his hair, something Ren had seen her do a hundred times. "I knew you'd be good with the Returner," she said. "I'm glad it has kept you safe."

"How did you know it would work for me?" said Alex.

"You got your hands on it once when you were very young – and you blew out the windows in the apartment."

"Maggie!" Todtman repeated. "Are the Spells unguarded?"

She looked up at him and nodded. *So she does have them*, thought Ren. "Yes," Dr Bauer said, her voice hardening as she spoke. "We need to get them out of here. I'm not ready yet."

"Ready for what?" said Ren as they all turned to follow Dr Bauer down the next alley.

She didn't answer.

Alex rushed to catch up with his mom. "I missed you," he said, so softly that it was nearly drowned out by the steady beat of their footsteps.

And that she did answer. "Oh, Alex, I so wish you hadn't found me yet – but I missed you, too. I left little signs to let you know I was still thinking about you." Ren's mind flashed back to the Valley of the Kings, to an old name penciled into a sun-scorched logbook. "Because the truth is, I missed you every moment of the day."

She led them through the little village, leaving her head uncovered. The time for hiding was over. What they needed now was escape.

Alex felt a stinging bite on the soft flesh of his neck and slapped down hard. "Oh no," he said before he even saw the flattened sand fly on his palm. The flies were back.

"What they see, The Order sees," said Todtman, waving at the buzzing cloud.

They were approaching a row of three mud-brick huts on the very edge of the village. The walls were thick, painted a fading blue, and the heavy wooden shutters were closed.

"They'll see," said Alex. "I can create some wind. Maybe—"

"It's OK," said his mom. "Let them."

She pulled open the door of the first hut. "Inside," she said quickly, before turning to her son. "Keep them out, Alex."

He nodded and grabbed the scarab. A quick gust scattered their tiny pursuers as the friends – and family – piled inside and quickly closed the door.

"Uh, Mom," Alex said into the hot, heavy darkness inside. "Do you want it back? Your scarab?"

A gas lantern sparked to life and the growing flame revealed a quick smile on her face. "Not now, honeybear," she said. "But hurry."

Alex had always been embarrassed by his mom's pet names for him, but right now "honeybear" sounded pretty sweet. And then she threw back a dusty old rug that was very nearly the only furnishing in the hut. In the light of the lantern, Alex saw a door in the floor.

"What's—" began Ren, but Dr Bauer was already kneeling down and pulling the trapdoor up and back.

"Stay quiet and follow me," she said.

Alex heard Todtman throw the steel bolt behind

them, locking the heavy wooden door from the inside. The next thing Alex knew, he was following his mom down a rusty old ladder into darkness. Sandy clay hardened into sandstone as they climbed twelve feet straight down. The ladder ended. Alex was surprised to find himself in a tunnel nearly high enough to stand in. Stooping slightly, he followed the glow of his mom's lantern forward.

He heard Todtman slam the trapdoor behind them. Flecks of sand and clay rained down on Alex's head as the others waddled forward like ducklings in the dark. The tunnel seemed none too stable, but Alex felt safer and more at ease than he had in weeks.

Twenty-odd yards later, they arrived at a second ladder. *The second hut*, Alex realized. His mom ignored this ladder, shimmying around it in the narrow tunnel and continuing on.

Finally, they reached the third ladder and ascended towards the third and final hut. "How did you dig all of this?" he huffed at his mom's back as they climbed.

"Most of the work was done a long time ago," she answered. "These huts were built over an old dig site here."

"When you were in school?" said Alex.

"Yes. We left them here as a way to ensure our claim of the site."

She threw back the trapdoor above them. By the time Alex climbed out, the room was already beginning to glow with the soft light of a larger lantern hanging from the ceiling.

The others emerged from the ground like desert gophers and Alex began to look around the hut's one shadowy room. There was a desk, a cot, a pitcher of water, an old trunk and a backpack leaning against the wall. He didn't see the Spells, but he felt them. His heart was racing and his head was buzzing. Pinpoints and whirls of light played at the edges of his vision.

"Is this what it feels like when you drink those huge coffees?" he asked.

Now and then the swirling lights coalesced into a hieroglyphic symbol. A glowing ankh, the loop-topped cross that meant life, formed in front of Alex. It seemed so real that he reached out for it, but there was nothing there.

"What are you doing?" said Ren.

"You didn't see that?"

"See what?"

"The Lost Spells gave you life," said his mom, once again kneeling down. "You are reacting to them."

She opened the lid of the old trunk and took out a square of black leather. Through the swirls, Alex recognized it as a briefcase his mom used to bring to work for important meetings. She lifted it free and carried it across the room. As she placed it down on the desk and clicked both brass clasps open – *tik! tik!* – Alex felt the sudden need to sit down. He looked around for a chair. There was only one, and it was tucked under the desk.

His mom opened the briefcase and Alex peered inside through a Milky Way's worth of stars. He saw a thin sheet of linen, covered in more hieroglyphs.

"Are those the Lost Spells?" asked Ren.

"No," said Dr Bauer. "These are the protective spells concealing them. Hiding their signal while I . . . studied them."

"You have been looking for a way to undo the damage," said Todtman, suddenly understanding. "To close the doorways without. . ."

They both turned their eyes to Alex and saw him swaying like a sapling in a windstorm.

"Yes," she said. "I have been looking for some way

to undo the damage the Spells have caused without undoing the magic that healed my son. But now I have run out of time." She took one more look at Alex, whose buzzing brain was able to form only one simple thought: *Why does she look so sad?*

"Watch him, please," she said.

And then she lifted the cloth.

Alex saw a slice of yellow light spread outward like a slow smile.

And then he fainted, dead away.

DEATH ON THE DOORSTEP

Alex had seen the pitcher of water in the corner of the room; he just hadn't expected to end up wearing it.

"Puhh!" he said, spluttering some of the water running down his face.

He reached up and wiped his eyes clear with his forearm, and there was Ren, towering above him holding the dripping pitcher. *Towering* was not a word normally associated with his vertically challenged friend, and that's when he realized he was on the floor.

"We have to go," Ren said apologetically.

He sat up and looked for his mom, with the sudden panicked thought that maybe he'd dreamed the whole thing. But the soreness from his fall told him how real this was, and then he spotted her over by the desk. She was carefully folding the linen wrapping back over the Lost Spells in her briefcase.

A powerful image flashed through his mind: his mom, sitting at that little desk, sipping her favourite tea and intensely studying the ancient Spells. Looking for some loophole, some shaded meaning in the hieroglyphic writing that would let her thread the needle, closing the doorways she'd opened to the afterlife without shutting the door on his own new life. *She has always taken care of me*, he thought.

Alex's mind returned to the here and now, and he noticed a small lump under the symbol-covered cloth. He hadn't seen that the first time. *Did she just put something in there with the Spells?* He sat up higher for a better look, but as he did, she slammed the briefcase closed and turned to him.

"Are you OK, hun?" she said. "Because we really do have to go."

He gave a woozy, bobbleheaded nod. He was OK-ish.

"Come out now! And bring the Spells!" called an all-too-familiar voice. "You are completely surrounded and there will be no escape."

Alex stiffened at the sound of Aff Neb's edgy voice. But the voice wasn't as loud as he expected: clearly shouted, but at a distance.

"Where are they?" said Alex, rising shakily to his feet.

Todtman was standing against the wall, peering out a narrow crack in the wooden shutter covering the front window. "They have the hut entirely surrounded," he said. "But it's the wrong hut."

Alex walked over to the window. With the Spells fully covered and the briefcase closed, his revving system had settled down somewhat. Todtman stepped aside and Alex peered through the crack.

Aff Neb looked to be about the size of an action figure, standing close to sixty yards away and bellowing threats at the first hut – the one they'd exited through the door in the floor. A squad of rifle-wielding gunmen surrounded the modest structure, looking like army action figures at this distance. Every once in a while, the swarming flies all around them coalesced into a visible pocket of blackness in the air before spreading out again and disappearing from view.

"They won't wait long," said Todtman.

Alex nodded absently. He was assessing the gunmen.

They had led The Order straight to his mom – and the Spells. They had made the ultimate mistake – *But maybe if it comes to a fight*, he thought, *we can win*. They had three amulets, and the presence of his mom seemed to add to their strength.

But then a man appeared who changed the maths. He walked straight out of the desert heat haze, his golden mask glinting in the sun. Alex's breath caught and he jumped back from the window.

"The leader is here, too," he said.

He said it to no one in particular, but his mom turned suddenly towards him. "*He's* here?" she said.

He stared at her, too surprised to answer. The tone of her voice – familiar, fearful – made it seem like she'd met the leader before. *But when? Where?* He had spent his whole life with her – just the two of them – but there was so much about his mom he didn't know...

The leader's voice stretched across the open desert, sounding like a whisper in Alex's ears but a

210

barked command in his head. "There is something wrong – step aside!"

The command was meant for the gunmen, but the leader's presence was so powerful that Alex had the urge to step aside himself. He fought it and took one last peek between the shutters.

There was a thick crunch of wood as the leader splintered the front door with a wave of his hand and walked unhindered into the hut. Alex watched as the gunmen streamed inside. He pictured them all, rifles pointed at every corner of the empty room. In a moment, they would find the trapdoor.

A more immediate sound tore his attention from the front window. It was the sound of the shutters being thrown open on the back window.

"We can climb out here," said his mom, ducking down to stuff the briefcase into her backpack. "They will try the second hut next – maybe split their forces and send some down into the tunnel."

"We have a car," said Todtman. "Back in the centre of the village."

Dr Bauer shook her head. "I have a truck," she said. "And it's closer." Then she boosted herself up and out of the window with the grace of a cat burglar.

As the friends rushed over to the open window

to help boost the old, decidedly graceless German out next, Ren turned to Alex. "Uh, your mom kind of kicks butt," she said.

Alex didn't know what to say. He'd always known his mom made a mean grilled cheese, but this? "I guess so," he managed. Then they both knelt down and laced their hands together for Todtman to step on.

Ren was too short to boost herself out the window, so Alex was the last one out. He plopped down on to the sandy ground on the shady side of the little shelter. His mom looked back at him, and once again he saw the familiar worry lines crease the corners of her eyes. He didn't like it. He knew he'd given her those lines in the first place. And now she was worried about him again. After all the trouble he'd caused. After he'd left his own cousin in a desert cell. After he'd led The Order right to her...

"It's all my fault," he whispered to her. "Everything that's happened, it's because of me. I put you in danger." His eyes flicked around the huddled group. "I put you all in danger."

His mom gave him a sad look. "Oh, hun, don't."

"It's true," he said, barely able to look her in the eyes.

She took his chin in her hand to make him. "No," she said. "It's not."

When he still wouldn't meet her eyes, she began to talk, her voice soft and warm. "We all had a choice," she said. "I chose to save you in that hospital room. I knew there was a risk, and I took it. The only thing you are responsible for is what you did after you woke up. And you came looking for me – to make things right. And that" – she gave his chin a shake – "that makes me proud."

"We had a choice, too," whispered Ren. "That's what I was trying to tell you leaving that pit. It's *not* all your fault – and we're not all your responsibility. We *all* had a choice."

Alex looked over at her, sceptical.

"I *chose* to come halfway around the world," she said, pointing at her own chest. As clear and firm as her statement was, it was her next words that convinced him. Flashing the quickest of grins she added: "Since when do I do what you tell me, anyway?"

Alex crouched in the sand, trying to process it all, replaying the words of the two people he trusted most. "We all had a choice," he said, turning it over in his head. He felt a weight lift, a burden ease. "I guess I can live with that."

His mom smiled, but just briefly. "Not if we don't get moving," she said, reaching over to ruffle his hair. "Now let's go! We should go straight ahead. Stay in the cover of the buildings as long as we can. The truck isn't far."

A voice carried across the desert. "Not here!" called the leader. "Check the next one!"

Alex's mom stopped to listen to the commanding voice, and for once Alex couldn't identify the look on her face. But as the voice fell silent, her determination returned. "They're heading for the second hut," she said, rising from her crouch. "Ready to run?"

Alex took one last look down at the cool, sheltering shade before heading out into the dangers of the open desert. But something was wrong. The ground wasn't shaded grey any more; it was glowing a rosy pink.

"Don't go," came a thin, scratchy voice. "Stay a while."

Alex knew who he would find even before he looked up.

Peshwar. The three-hut shell game had fooled the rest of them, but The Order's heartless huntress had sniffed them out.

She stood waiting for them ten feet away, gazing out through the eye sockets of the sun-bleached lioness skull. In her hand was a shimmering crimson energy dagger. As soon as he saw it, Alex's elbow ached at the memory of its bite.

Quick as a whip, the hand holding the bloodred dagger shot back and rocketed forward. Alex and Ren dived to one side, Todtman and Bauer dropped to the other, and the brutal projectile slammed into the wall between them with a loud, crackling explosion.

Alex felt little chunks of mud brick spray across the back of his shirt, but what worried him more was the sound. He knew that would carry much farther – and alert the rest of The Order's forces.

As he rolled over and popped to his feet, Alex heard the shouts of men on the move and the metallic clicks and shucks of rifles being readied for action. The hunters were on the way. If the friends were to escape, if they were to keep the limitless power of the Spells out of the hands of their pursuers, it would have to be now.

We all have a choice, thought Alex, *and I choose to fight*.

Alex's hand closed tightly around the scarab, the beetle's wings digging into his palm, just a hint of the pain and danger to come. He turned to face the lethal lioness.

Peshwar lowered her hand and another energy dagger formed, spreading downward and crackling with power. Like an Old West gunfighter, Alex knew she was faster on the draw than he was. But her hand was still down, and his was already on the way up. He pointed his fingers like a spear.

The concentrated gust shot outward with the power of ten sledgehammers, but this time it was Peshwar who ducked nimbly to the side. Her crimson robes fluttered as she tucked and rolled across the sand. In an instant she was up – and releasing her dagger!

It flew not towards Alex, but straight at Todtman. And the old man was not nearly as nimble.

"No!" shouted Alex.

Todtman had one hand on his amulet and the other on his broom-handle cane. Too late and too slow to duck, he swung the cane like a baseball bat. Germans are not known for their baseball prowess, but somehow the awkward swing connected. The wood exploded in his hand.

Todtman released a sputtering shout of pain – "Aaghkk!" – and went down in a heap.

Alex couldn't tell how badly he was hurt – and had no time to ask. He spread his fingers wider to make his next gust harder to dodge. But before he released it, he took a quick look to make sure his mom and Ren were out of the way.

And that's when Ren released another powerful flash of white light. Not looking at her and with her eyes shielded by the sockets of her skull mask, Peshwar barely seemed to notice. Alex, on the other hand, had been standing in the shade and looking directly at it.

"Gaah!" he blurted, suddenly blinded.

And so he only heard the flies descend.

Millions of them.

The living, swarming cloud of hard-shelled bodies and beating wings felt as thick and tumultuous as breaking waves at the beach.

Alex knew the stakes now, understood the sort of ancient power and modern malice they faced. They were fighting not just for their own lives but for the fate of the world itself.

And that fight was not going well.

The insects engulfed him – swarming, biting – and the only sound louder than their buzzing was the burning crackle of the approaching energy dagger.

THE TIDES OF WAR

Alex was pushed hard to the ground a moment before the energy dagger arrived, taking another chunk out of the wall behind him. He landed facedown, knocking the air from his lungs. He gasped to replace it and sucked in sand – but that was still better than a mouthful of flies. He could feel them swarming all around. He didn't even dare open his eyes to see who had saved him.

The sand flies bit down at the freshly exposed skin on the back of his neck. And the smell was

219

almost worse. The energy dagger had bug-zapped a wide swath of them as it passed. The scent of so many barbecued bugs made him want to retch.

The scarab, he thought. *At least I can whip up some wind and get rid of these bloodthirsty pests.*

But as he reached up for the amulet, he found nothing. He patted his neck and chest furiously. *Oh no oh no oh no!* He reached around to the back of his bug-ravaged neck. He realized in horror that the worst sting he'd felt hadn't been a sting at all. It had been the raking scrape of the silver chain being torn free.

"Don't let her use it!" he heard. "Don't let her put it on!"

There was a rapid-fire barrage of energy daggers – *crackle, crash, boom* – and then there was a louder sound.

Much louder.

KRRAKOOOOM!

The thunder was so close overhead that it shook Alex's teeth. Just as he was scrambling to his feet, a vicious wind shear knocked him back to the ground. Suddenly, the flies were gone, and the rain began to pour down.

Alex opened his eyes into a downpour.

Lightning crackled overhead.

His mom had the scarab back.

The Order operatives had failed. He looked on in awe as she stood tall between him and his attackers. He had managed to summon the wind that came before the rain with the scarab. She had brought the rain itself.

Ren rushed over to him. "Are you OK?" she said through the lashing wind and rain.

Alex felt the smashed bodies of the bugs he'd managed to swat sliding off of him in the rain. "I think so," he said. "Look!"

In front of them, Todtman climbed back to his feet. Alex caught a glimpse of his eyes: They had changed. They looked like two glittering gems, the eyes of his falcon amulet writ large.

He stood shoulder to shoulder with Alex's mom, the wind rippling the back of his white shirt.

Peshwar and Aff Neb took a look at each other and then a shaky step back. Alex and Ren were novice Amulet Keepers, still trying to figure out what the scarab and ibis could do, but in front of them stood two Amulet Keepers in full. They seemed to be feeding off of each other's power, and the Egyptian sky roared its approval.

KRAKOOOOM!

As a flash of yellow lit the dark clouds overhead, Alex felt a glimmer of hope. The Order lieutenants were intimidated, almost transfixed by the display of power, but the spell was broken by a half dozen gunmen rushing around the perimeter of the old hut.

Dr Bauer turned towards the new threat. The men pointed their rifles but then threw them to the ground and dived for cover. Alex hadn't been holding a chunk of metal, but he felt the sudden electrical charge in the air, too. He grabbed Ren and they sheltered against the battered wall.

This time the lightning hit the open ground near the prone gunmen. They flopped and convulsed like fish on a skillet before rolling over and hugging themselves in pain. Sand is a natural insulator, but the ground was wet, and even though he was farther from the strike, Alex's mouth tingled like he'd been sucking on a battery. He turned to Ren to find her formerly rain-slick black hair puffed out in all directions like an oversized dandelion.

Aff Neb rushed forward to attack. But before he'd made it three steps, he was attacking *himself*! His fists took turns punching his own head. Alex winced as he saw Aff Neb's left fist land smack-dab in his bulbous right eye. Todtman's jewel-like eyes gleamed as he guided the beat-down.

Peshwar tried her luck, flicking her hand down to summon another energy dagger. But almost as soon as the glow appeared, the red energy began to flicker and snap in her rain-slick hand. Even with the sky as dark as grey wool, Alex could see her eyes behind the sockets of the lioness skull, staring unblinking at his mom.

Ren saw it, too. Standing behind and a little to the left of Alex's mom, she raised her hand and pointed her fingers. Alex looked down and away.

FWOOOOP!

The brilliant white light filled the dark day – and Peshwar's unblinking eyes.

"Daa!" she spluttered, and as she did, the energy dagger fizzled out in her hand.

After one more punch to his own jaw, Aff Neb dropped to the ground a few steps in front of his soggy, blinded comrade. Twenty yards to the side, the gunmen still writhed in pain as their guns sizzled on the wet sand.

In a matter of minutes, the tides of war had shifted dramatically. Alex pushed himself free of the old wall, which was suddenly less brick and more mud, and looked around at a battle that seemed won. Joy and relief, strangers to him for so long, began to take hold.

But not all their enemies were accounted for.

The leader walked slowly into view. His thick ceremonial robes trailed just a few inches above the rain-soaked ground, but his body language gave the distinct impression of being far above it all. In the dim light of the storm, his golden vulture mask looked tarnished and fearsome. The iron beak was a pure, slick black. Alex's lungs filled to shout a warning. But before he could, he found himself frozen.

He could only stare at his mom's back as she and Todtman turned their attention to Peshwar. The mighty huntress now looked like a sullen, wet cat, her long-nailed hands held out like claws and her robes clinging to her skeletally thin frame.

Turn around! Alex thought as hard as he could. *Behind you!*

In thrall to the leader's power, he desperately wished he could move – then suddenly, he *was* moving.

And then he desperately wished he could stop.

His feet carried him forward. At first his steps were thick and awkward, but he sped up as the leader became more accustomed to his newest instrument. Next to him, Ren was doing the same thing. Or rather the same thing was being done to her. Alex heard her footfalls in the wet sand.

No no no! he thought.

But there was no denying it. They were running directly towards the others. He could feel his breathing, mechanical and even, but couldn't harness it to say even a single word. *Look out, Mom,* he thought. *Look out!*

But it wasn't his thoughts she heard. It was his wet, slapping footsteps.

Still focused on Peshwar, she risked a quick look back.

Too late.

Alex felt his legs sink lower and – *NO!* – launch him through the air.

As he flew towards his mom, he felt the leader's iron grip slip. He did everything he could to soften the blow, curling back in on himself in midair, but it was too late. He hit his mom in the midsection with a flying body block that knocked her to the ground with a muddy splash. Her hand came off the scarab as she reached out instinctively to protect not herself but her son from the impact.

Todtman saw Ren approaching, but he didn't understand the threat. "Ren?" he said, the jewel-like glow fading from his eyes. Then she launched herself – despite herself – and hit him low. He yelped like a kicked dog as she ploughed into his bad leg, and they both went down hard.

The thunder faded and the rain stopped.

"I'm sorry! I'm sorry! I'm sorry!" said Alex, rolling over. The four of them had fallen into a lumpy heap on the ground, and were now turning and twisting as they began to disentangle themselves and sit up. He looked over to see if his mom was hurt or mad. "I couldn't help it!"

Instead of anger on her face, he saw a flash of confusion give way to a steadier glow. A rosy red light washed over her. She reached for the scarab, but stopped halfway as the point of a fresh energy dagger extended down almost to her nose.

"Don't," purred Peshwar.

And as the unnatural clouds pulled apart above them and the strong desert sun shone through, a second shadow fell across them.

The leader surveyed the wreckage wordlessly.

Alex heard the sound of the trapdoor popping open inside the hut. Almost immediately, the remaining gunmen rushed out like ants from a shattered anthill. They pointed their rifles down at the fallen Amulet Keepers.

"The Spells, please," said the leader, breaking the heavy silence.

"We don't have them," said Todtman, sitting up and seemingly daring the gunmen to shoot.

The leader looked over. "Who do you think you're talking to, Ernst?" he said.

Ren was on Todtman's left and Alex caught her eye and mouthed one word: *Ernst?*

"I know exactly who I am talking to," replied Todtman.

"Then you know you cannot lie to me," said the leader. He searched Todtman's face and seemed to find something there. He turned towards Dr Bauer. "The backpack, please."

"Mom, don't!" called Alex, but she was already taking her backpack off, already handing it over. He could see the square edges of the briefcase through the nylon.

One of the gunmen reached down and took the pack. Alex glared at him as he ripped the top open and removed the briefcase. "Bring it to me," said the leader.

Alex looked around desperately, seeking some means of escape. But they were surrounded by enemies. The leader's eyes gleamed beneath his mask as the gunmen held the case out flat for him to open.

"Are they in there?" came a familiar voice. The smell as much as the tone told Alex that Aff Neb was back on his feet and approaching.

"Yes," said the leader. "I can feel their power."

Alex turned to his mom, ready to follow her lead. Instead, he saw her hand slip down towards her pants pocket.

Pop-pop!

The leader popped the clasps, and all eyes, even Peshwar's, shifted to the briefcase. Only Alex watched as his mom slid a plastic baggie from her pocket and removed a small black device from inside.

His pulse revved and his head swam as the leader slowly opened the case. But he was determined to stay conscious this time. Something was happening. An image flashed through his mind: *His mom folding the protective linen wrapping back over the Lost Spells, a small lump just visible...*

The lump was some sort of explosive charge. His mom would destroy the Spells rather than hand them over!

"There's something in here!" said the leader, alarmed. He pulled back the linen and Alex swayed and swooned. If he hadn't already been sitting in the wet sand, he was pretty sure he would've fallen over. But despite the powerful effect of the uncovered Spells, he fought to keep his fluttering eyes open.

His mom raised the little remote.

Press it, he thought. *Press it now!*

But she hesitated. Just for a second. Alex watched as she flexed her thumb without pressing down – and then the chance was lost.

The leader saw it now. He held out one hand, palm up, and the little device tore free from Maggie's grasp and flew to him. He cradled it gently as it arrived, catching it as if it were an egg. A moment later, it disappeared into the folds of his dark robes.

"Take their amulets," he said.

Alex watched woozily as Peshwar plucked the scarab from his mom and Aff Neb took Todtman's falcon and Ren's ibis. Alex bowed his head, helpless and beaten. The leader watched them carefully until the amulets were secured. Then he grabbed a small silver box from the briefcase and tossed it into the sand.

"Incendiary device," he said as it landed with a soft thud. Taking a long, hungry look at the Spells, he added, "They're beautiful."

He covered them back up and snapped the case shut. With the Spells once again concealed, Alex's head began to clear. He leaned towards his mom and whispered, "Why didn't you press it?"

She dropped her head. "I couldn't."

"She spent her whole life searching for them," interrupted the leader, his booming voice seeming to mock their whispers. "The greatest find in the history of archaeology. Not an easy thing to destroy."

"And instead," she said, staring down at the sand, "I have destroyed the world."

"Don't be so dramatic, Maggie," he said. The last word echoed through Alex's mind like one final peal of thunder. *Maggie. . . Who was this man who knew both Todtman and his mom?* "The world will not be destroyed in the Final Kingdom. It will be reborn. You, of all people, should understand that."

Alex's mom finally looked up at the man who mocked her. "A living death, then, ruled by tyrants."

Her tone was so sad and defeated that it tore

Alex's heart in half. "It's not your fault," he said to her, trying anything to make her feel less miserable. "He made me run into you. I couldn't help myself."

Alex's mom looked over at him, her eyes softening even as the old worry lines deepened. "I thought I told you," she said. "Don't blame yourself."

"No, don't," said the leader, continuing to intrude on the conversation. "You did as I wished, but then, a boy should obey his father."

Alex stared at the man. *"What?"* he heard Ren say. Alex tore his eyes from the leader and looked back to his mom for confirmation.

"Alex, honey . . ." she began, but she didn't seem to know where to go from there. A moment later, the time for talk was over. They were prodded to their feet at gunpoint. Alex felt a rifle barrel digging into his back and reluctantly complied.

A few feet away, he saw Ren help Todtman to his feet. The friends were wet and battered and bowed in defeat.

Alex looked back at the leader, this man who claimed to be his father, this man whose face he'd still never seen. This man who'd been ready to sacrifice him in that pit. Alex wondered if he'd kill them all now.

The Order had everything: the amulets and their Keepers; the Lost Spells and their power. The Death Walkers would return; the stone warriors would rise. There was no force left in the world that could stop them.

Alex felt the gun barrel dig into his back again.

He shuffled slowly forward. What else could he do?

HIEROGLYPHIC ALPHABET

A	J	SH
B	K	T
C	L	TH
CH	M	U
D	N	V
E	O	W
F	P	X
G	Q	Y
H	R	Z
I	S	